With b, *^1 June 2025* *Esther,* *he*

Rose's

Tales of love and loss

"Fascinating, poignant, and beautifully told glimpses of the relationships, regrets, and heartaches of ordinary people."

- Siân Harris, Writer

SANGITA SWECHCHA

Translated by

JAYANT SHARMA

Cover design: P. Singh
Cover photo: Rhoslyn Singh
Published Date: April 2024
Published by: Book Hill International

ISBN: 978-1-915159-06-9

Website: www.bookhill.co.uk
Email: info@bookhill.co.uk

Praise for Rose's Odyssey

"I must admit that this book carries a substantial literary weight and serves as a valuable addition to Nepali literature, establishing itself as a noteworthy literary work."
- *Tulasi Diwasa, Legendary Writer*

"Swechcha masterfully weaves her narratives and imaginations into a patchwork of words. Each story resembles a finely crafted sketch, brought to life through the art of words."
- *Mani Lohani, Writer, Madhuparka Literary Magazine*

"The stories within the book defy the reader's initial assumptions. Numerous narratives hold unexpected twists that catch readers off guard, adding a layer of intrigue and highlighting the captivating essence of Sangita's storytelling."
- *Shekhar Kharel, Writer and Documentary Filmmaker*

"The author has adeptly crafted these stories, which address the themes of harrowing economic and psychological hardships, the daunting uncertainty of the future, the struggles of identity, the realisation of one's minority status, the quest for existence, and a deep connection to the past."
- *Susmita Nepal, Writer, The Global Circle Journal, Tribhuvan University*

"The effort to contribute organic stories of the occidental world to Nepali literature from a diasporic land is especially laudable as not many books in fiction have come out from this sector."
- Prava Baral, Writer, Online Khabar

"'Rose's Odyssey' stands out as a highly symbolic and my personal favourite piece. This story weaves parallels between a blooming rose in front of the protagonist's house and his romantic relationship, infusing it with both sentiment and romance. The remaining nineteen stories in the collection are equally captivating."
- Bijaya Hitan, Writer

"The author's writing exhibits a sharp edge, allowing her stories to serve as poignant critiques of the deformities and disparities prevalent in society. These stories are skilfully constructed through a thoughtful blend of diverse social classes, settings, events, and characters."
- Arun Khatri Nadi, Shabdankur Literary Magazine

"This collection features stories that eloquently depict the joys and sorrows within women's hearts. The stories illuminate the constricted mindset and ego of men, as well as feminist perspectives and selfishness, effectively conducting an incisive examination of our society."
- Krishna Bajgain, Samakalin Sahitya

"While these stories are works of fiction, they are firmly rooted in reality. In each of Dr. Sangita's stories, you can find reflections of both worlds."
- Subash Singh Parajuli, Writer, Saurya Online

"The collection beautifully weaves together the tales of Nepali immigrants, exploring their complex mind set, nostalgia, challenges of living abroad, vulnerability, aspirations, conflicts, feminist perspectives, regrets, love, jealousy, repentance, sacrifice, dreams, and anxieties."
- *Khusi Limbu, NepalBritain.com*

"I've evaluated this collection as a testament to her success in doing justice to characters of all kinds."
- *Sanuraja Anjaan, Writer, Shabdapath*

"This collection underscores Sangita Swechcha's talent for minutely examining the emotional nuances within women's hearts. The stories primarily centre on personal themes such as love, dedication, friendship, bitterness, betrayal, struggle, success, and failure, all while adeptly portraying the deformity of male ego and their narrow mindset."
- *Jay Prakash Tripathi, Editor, Ghatana Ra Bichar Weekly*

"The collection of 20 stories titled 'Rose's Odyssey' serves as a reflection of figurative narratives. The collection's title, derived from the first story within it, stands out as a milestone work among the others in the volume."
- *Online Khabar*

"Whether it's the impact of diverse cultures and environments, the fallout from rumours, or the betrayals and malice in the commercial arena, author Swechcha has adeptly wielded her pen to hold up a mirror to society, revealing its inner workings."
- *Suresh Jung Shah, Writer, Samakalin Sahitya*

"I had the pleasure of reading Dr. Sangita Swechcha's short story collection 'The Rose's Odyssey.' Thanks to its intriguing event descriptions, intricate plots, and engaging writing style, my affection has been drawn particularly not to the rose, but to these extraordinary stories."
- *Ramlal Joshi, Award-winning Author*

"The ebb and flow between stories was different every time, some leading straight into the next while others needing space to sit and linger. A wonderful insight into cultural differences on a highly personal and intimate level."
- *Jessica Hayden, Editor*

Journey Across Borders and Emotions

When Sangita told me she'd written a new book, my first question was whether she would consider publishing an English language version. I'm delighted that she listened to this request!

This new edition brings the diverse collection of stories to a wider audience. It gives readers a fascinating, poignant, and beautifully told glimpses of the relationships, regrets, and heartaches of ordinary people in Nepal, Australia and the UK.

From whimsical, rose-inspired musings about lost loves to troubled teens, these stories allow us to peek into other lives.

Particularly interesting to me were the diaspora vignettes set in the UK, drawing on the author's own travel experiences and sharp observational skills.

- Siân Harris, Writer, England

Contents

Rose's Odyssey

As usual, the bush next to my house remained silent—almost like a personification of melancholy. The sun rose in the bush just as it did in my front garden. However, the rose nestled within that bush appeared sad. Perhaps she was unhappy about the abundance of beautiful flowers in my garden, considering roses were often regarded as the most beautiful. However, my garden lacked roses, while chrysanthemums and snapdragons bloomed abundantly. I diligently tended to them every day, which might have explained their flourishing beauty.

I believed the rose would have been delighted if I could have relocated her from the bush to my garden. Unfortunately, I was unable to do so. The dense bush was surrounded by nettles, enclosing the moon-like pink rose at its core. She appeared teary-eyed, as if afflicted by a distressing solitude, with her lashes soaked in tears. Despite her delicate youthful appearance, it seemed like she was making an extra effort to showcase her beauty from within the bush. After all, she must have had numerous desires to flaunt her beauty to everyone. I stood captivated, observing all this from the east-facing window of the house. Suddenly, dark clouds overshadowed the glaring sun, hinting at an imminent downpour. I became agitated, fearing that the rain would harm the rose.

"Biraj! Hey, Biraj!" Sharmila Didi[1]'s voice interrupted my contemplation. I turned around.

"Yes, Didi!" I quickly replied. She was surprised to see her brother in tears. Since childhood, her love for me had been unconditional, and I considered myself fortunate to have her in my life.

"Why do you have tears in your eyes?" she exclaimed as she approached me.

"It's not my tears, Didi, but the rose's!" I inadvertently got carried away.

"You're silly! Make sure the milk doesn't get cold." She walked away, leaving a glass of milk beside me. It wasn't that I enjoyed drinking milk, but due to a bout of fever, I had to consume it.

Lost in my thoughts, I immersed myself in the world of the rose. I became engulfed in a sea of fantasy. I closed my eyes and took a deep breath—daydreaming. Even in my dreams, I remained as Biraj. I walked towards the rose, realising that the bush was not as dense. I wished I could call her by name, but since I didn't know it, my lips quivered unknowingly. She smiled at me, and I felt elated. The surroundings suddenly bustled with activity. With a smile, she called out, "Biraj!"

Surprised and overwhelmed with happiness, I took hesitant steps towards her. Simultaneously, I felt a sense of caution about her voice.

[1] *Elder sister*

2

"Biraj! Feel me once, and I will provide answers to all your curiosities about what you will discover within me."

Her feeble voice resonated heavily in my mind, evoking a sense of familiarity that propelled me forward with confidence. I didn't just want to experience her presence; I desired to hold her in my heart. But plucking her? No, that would be akin to committing a murder. I couldn't bear to harm her for a momentary pleasure. Instead, I yearned to engage in hours of conversation with her, exploring the depths of our relationship through this silent language. Poor thing! She must have endured the harsh treatment of frosty nights, foggy days, and relentless monsoon rains. From now on, I vowed not to let anything disturb her. I would offer her my utmost love and protection.

Lost in these thoughts, I failed to realise how close I had come to her. The closer I got, the more breathtaking she appeared.

"Biraj!" She suddenly screamed, and instinctively, my hands reached out to hold her. In that moment, I saw Rubina in her.

Excited, I woke up from my dream. Dusk was approaching, and as I rubbed my eyes, I glanced out the window. The road was muddy, and the garden was drenched in water. What if the beloved rose was battered by the shower? Fear consumed me. The muddy road was a consequence of Didi's son leaving the hose on. It was an unusual dream, yet it had transported me to the realm of reality. Memories of the past surged in my mind. Rubina... the same radiant and vibrant Rubina whom I first met in

Dharan. When I left for Kathmandu, she shed countless tears, yet I never wrote back to her.

Today, I was quite amazed. Thousands of people walked along the road each day, yet no one noticed the rose in the bush, let alone understood her pain. Such is human nature—longing for something esteemed and overlooking the hidden gem suffocating beneath a bush. It was only recently that I too noticed her. Perhaps she had been peeking out from the bush when Didi and I had a bet a few days ago about the beauty of chrysanthemums in our garden. How hurt the rose must have felt at that time!

Nevertheless, I decided to relocate her to our front garden, where I could freely converse with her. Would she address me by my name as she did in my dreams? If not, I would still revel in her presence and relish her fragrance. If not for my fever, I would have joyfully leaped off the wall and cleared the bush by now. But it was due to this fever that I stood brooding at the window and that's how I happened to catch sight of her. I had never noticed her during my journeys to and from college, only recently because of my illness. I yearned to alleviate the sadness that overshadowed her delicate face.

For the past three days, my mind had been consumed by one thing. After all, the culmination of beauty lay hidden within that bush. I refused to see myself defeated. I couldn't imagine finding happiness if her existence were in vain. I would not let my confidence waver.

***

I recovered from my fever and successfully relocated the rose to our garden in front of my window. The sight of the rose reminded me of Rubina, bringing me back to the harsh reality. Happiness overwhelmed me, and a desire to win both the rose and Rubina ignited within me. Urgently, I set off for Dharan[2]. However, despite the immense excitement with which I arrived, I was met with an equal measure of sadness. I failed to grasp the weight of Rubina's tears, nor did I attempt to understand it. Consequently, she couldn't comprehend my pain either.

Upon reaching Dharan, the waves of my happiness were abruptly halted. It was Rubina's wedding, and I witnessed her farewell with my own eyes. It felt unreal, yet it was the bitter reality. I felt as if I had insulted myself, and my confidence was shattered. When I opened my closed eyes, it was too late. The wedding had already taken place, and she belonged to someone else. I wanted to cry my heart out, but I restrained myself. With tearful eyes, I somehow managed to return home after three days. Upon returning, I yearned to touch the rose just for once and repent… for the sake of the tears shed by Rubina.

***

Yes! I had been cursed by Rubina's tears. I erased her from my life. On one hand, Rubina became a stranger, and on the other hand, the petals of the rose, which constantly reminded me of Rubina, kept falling to the ground.

---

[2] *Dharan, a city located in eastern Nepal, is approximately 250 miles by road from Kathmandu, the capital city.*

Perhaps the rosebush was its rightful place. I made a mistake by bringing her into my flower garden. It pained me… My heart shattered into pieces. I felt the urge to mend the rose petals… But it was impossible! Those fallen petals mocked my current state of misery. Sleep eluded me at night. I collected the fallen rose petals and took them to my room.

The past with Rubina started replaying like a movie in my mind. I struggled to hold myself together. The wrong that my ex-girlfriend, Sarita, had done to me, I sought revenge on Rubina, and the only one who suffered in the end was that rose. Sarita, whether knowingly or unknowingly, caused me trouble. I despised the selfish and callous nature of women. My disgust extended beyond Sarita to all women. It felt like fragility was being ridiculed in the name of femininity. Only because Sarita made me an object of ridicule, I retaliated against Rubina. But Rubina wept bitterly the day she had to leave me… I understood that a single tear of a woman is a powerful weapon that weakens men. So, I disregarded her tears, consoling myself and mocking them, believing that I hadn't let my masculinity falter. A woman betrayed me… something my ego couldn't bear.

To bow down before a woman as a man? No… Instead, I made Rubina cry. Her tears soothed my fiery masculine heart. I went to Dharan and made promises… only to forget them upon arriving in Kathmandu. At that time, I had only one purpose. To seek revenge on a woman… on the entire female race. What did I gain in return? My heart became a battleground of prolonged pain. The tears of remorse fought to find their way onto my soaked pillow, intensifying the restlessness within me.

What a shame! I have disappointed my entire race in front of women. But not all women are as wicked as Sarita, and not all men would respond to that wickedness as I did. Perhaps it was all predetermined in my fate, and I had to endure it.

My eyes began to ache, so I closed them and fell into a deep sleep, entering the realm of dreams. In my dreams, Rubina was speaking to me, saying, "Biraj... just consider me dead in this lifetime, but in the next life, I will be yours... Biraj... Biraj..."

I suddenly woke up, clutching the rose petals in my hand as if they understood my sorrow. Once my agitation settled, I released my grip. The petals had crumbled and formed a mass. My agitation grew even stronger. It felt as though along with the death of Rubina in my dreams, her memories had also died. I felt ashamed of myself. I had killed the rose. I had destroyed its life in my selfish desire to adorn my own garden. I no longer felt like staying at home. I didn't even have the chance for redemption. It would have been better if the rose had remained in that bush, at least I could have spoken to it, in memory of Rubina.

***

I grew weary of life. If I stayed home, this pain would always torment me. That's why I embarked on a trip to Kashmir[3] with my father, accompanying him on his work-trip. After three months, I returned home from Kashmir. I had almost forgotten my past, but there was a new rose bud blossoming on the rose plant in front of my window. She had the same beauty, the same colour, the same laughter, the same charm... She seemed to be eagerly awaiting my arrival. A tear of joy uncontrollably welled up in my eyes. I approached her with excitement. I longed to touch the rose in front of me, but I couldn't bring myself to do it. What if my touch took her life once again? Oh, on the windowsill above my bed head, the old rose petals had wilted and crumbled. I performed a symbolic cremation beneath the same rose plant in my front garden.

My hands still trembled. Restlessness had consumed me entirely. I abruptly woke up and gazed at that little rose... Resting in the same spot as the previous one, she said, "Biraj! I have been reborn. I am the same rose. I have been waiting for you all this time. Today, I am grateful for the place you have given me, which I always yearned for... You are great, Biraj... You have saved my existence. I was restless in the bush outside... Look, there is a tear of happiness in my eyes that you have bestowed upon me."

I extended my hand to gently wipe away the tear from the rose. In that moment, I disregarded the potential effect of my touch on the delicate flower. Closing my eyes briefly, I

---

[3] *Situated to the northwest of Kathmandu, Kashmir is approximately 560 miles away, separated by the diverse terrains of northern India.*

immersed myself in the memories of the past. I perceived the rose as Rubina herself, as if she were speaking to me: "Biraj! I have been reborn. Perhaps in my previous life, I was married to someone else, but in this life, we shall never be apart." Unaware that this emotional exchange existed solely within my imagination, I became suddenly excited and exclaimed, "Rubina has been reincarnated!"

However, upon opening my eyes, Rubina was nowhere to be found. I felt remorseful for my actions, but I attempted to make amends by becoming like a flower myself. When I became lost in my imagination, I transformed into a new rose and engaged in conversation, perceiving the little rose as Rubina. Even in reality, I consoled my heart by caring for the rose. I feared that I may erase her existence too. When I touched the little rose, it transformed into Rubina in my mind. Thus, the love story between the rose and myself began.

I vowed to protect our love from being destroyed. She was not Sarita; she was my Rubina. Even if she had once been married to someone else, she would remain in my front garden which I can watch regularly from my window. I would provide her with shelter during the monsoons and dress her in protective plastic during winters. When she shed tears, I would gently wipe them away. We would engage in hours-long conversations during the night, when everyone else in the house was asleep. I never wanted anyone to mock the love story between the rose and myself. Our love was genuine, true love.

Oh God! In another life, may I become a rose. I refuse to live separated from Rubina. After all, the bond between the rose and my love was sacred.

***

The Unknown Call

The constant barking of dogs breaks the silence and tranquillity of Barclay Road in Croydon town. The strong winds would leave flowers and leaves struck dead, and trees deracinated. However, Lily is seen furtively entering the house from the backdoor at this dead hour of the night. Perhaps Lily's mother will find answers to all her doubts today. She descends the stairway slowly, unwilling to accept in good faith her daughter warily entering the house on such a stormy night.

"Lily, where have you come from?"

There is no answer from Lily.

"Give me your mobile! This is what has messed you up!" Sajana tries to snatch the phone from her daughter. Lily crossly hands the phone to her mother and runs up the stairway to her bedroom without a word.

Sajana feels the urge to give Lily a piece of her mind but restrains her raging temper. She is equally concerned about her only daughter walking out of the house in contempt. Hers is an age that can create a fuss. Despite being fifteen, Lily appears older than her age, often mistaken for eighteen or more by those meeting her for the first time. Standing at 5 feet 8 inches tall with wide blue eyes, a milky complexion, and a beautiful facial structure, Lily's beauty is unparalleled in school. Her charming face, elegant soft voice, and polite demeanour attract the attention of many boys in her class. While it is not unusual for a fifteen-year-old girl to have a boyfriend in a country like England, Lily's Nepali mother has never been able to fathom this.

Lily's mother, Sajana, has been living in England for the past sixteen years. Sajana arrived in England after getting married to a British tourist, Bryan, whom she met in Nepal about seventeen years ago. On paper, Sajana is a British national but somewhere inside, she still feels a connection to her Nepali roots. It is not acceptable in her view for a fifteen-year-old girl to have a boyfriend.

The door to Lily's room is closed. The unceasing upheaval of the weather outside imbibes in Sajana a feeling of angst. Her daughter's silence adds to the situation. For quite a while, Sajana contemplates rummaging through Lily's mobile phone and laptop; however, Lily never leaves home without her belongings. It is natural for a mother to worry about her daughter's well-being. She wants to talk to Lily about her behaviour change and advise her on worldly virtues but, for Sajana, the right time is yet to come.

While the lights in Lily's room are still on, she has already surrendered to the bed without changing.

"Darling, are you asleep?" Sajana inquires, gently caressing Lily's hair. There is no response from Lily as she continues taking deep sighs in slumber.

Outside, the ruthless ferocity of the weather continues. The constant barking of dogs deports Sajana's mind to an unusual state of fear and inquisitiveness. Strangely, her street experiences a power outage for the first time in seventeen years. For Sajana, it is a moment of utter despair. She presses Lily's mobile phone with the hope of inviting dim brightness to the room. To her utter shock, there are twenty missed calls from an unknown number in the last fifteen minutes. Sajana contemplates waking Lily up and making things clear, but she is conflicted about whether or not to do that late at night.

"Doesn't a mother have the right to know about her daughter? Aren't I her mother?" Sajana ponders, staring constantly at her sleeping beauty.

People say Lily inherited those wide beautiful eyes and impeccable visage from her mother, but Sajana doesn't find herself that attractive. However, it is from her dad she inherited that imposing height and those mesmerising blue eyes.

In the meantime, the power is back. Sajana looks at herself in the mirror lying nearby. She sees her life as inexplicable. More than forty years old, she doesn't find her confidence growing at all with her advancing age. That should probably be one of the reasons why she is so reluctant to speak even with her daughter.

"A scaredy-cat you are! You are a mother who gave her birth and raised her, but you lag behind in taking up the responsibility." She is startled seeing her own reflection in the mirror. Many times, she gets disturbed by a solemn thought—like being a failed wife, what if she turns into a failed mother too!

Sajana looks in the mirror again and takes a deep breath. And then dials that unknown number on her mobile phone. Rather than waking Lily up and letting her call the number, Sajana feels it wiser to find it for herself. However, the call goes unanswered.

***

The mellow chirping of birds in the morning adds splendour to the air. The rooms are brightly lit with the early morning sun. Seeing nature in its utmost sanity, one would never envisage the severity of last night. It is hardly six in the morning.

"The flowers in the garden must have perished. Probably, a couple of trees must have fallen down too," Sajana is engrossed in her thoughts as she takes sips from the cup of tea in her hand.

Lily is still asleep. Sajana doesn't feel like going and checking her out either. More than the storm last night, Sajana is growing restless because of the storm hitting her heart now. She is rather concerned about the time Lily would get up so that she could ask her the reasons behind using the backdoor and those numerous missed calls on her phone.

The doorbell rings. The early morning chime startles Lily from her sleep. Sajana rushes to the door and is surprised to find a group of policemen standing outside.

"Perhaps Lily has done something! Is she doing drugs? Or maybe she was with some bad guy last night…?" A flood of doubts rushes through Sajana's mind.

"There was an accident in front of your house, and the driver is already dead. We need to ask you something about this."

"Oh my gosh! That's scary!" Sajana's voice is trembling, and her eyes start fluttering.

"Any chance you identify the dead? Can you please step out and have a look?"

"I don't expect I can! Who can it be? There are hundreds of cars on the streets." Sajana comes out of the house in slippers with the intent of helping the police. Lily follows her mother.

"The incident took place at around midnight. We could have saved him had we been informed in time!" The tallest of the officers informs.

Lily recognises the car from a distance. She runs to the car faster than the speed of the storm last night. Sajana follows her daughter, but Lily is already there, broken into tears as she looks inside the car.

Seeing a daughter cry, any mother in the world would feel bad. Sajana also cannot hold back her emotions.

"He must be Lily's boyfriend." Heaven forbids her doubts to come true! She can't, in her wildest dream, wish anything as such for anybody. She is, in fact, worried about her daughter now. Moreover, Lily's terrified yell clearly explains her closeness with the deceased. As Sajana comes closer to the car and peeps in, the glimpse beats the hell out of her. Lily is still crying her heart out while Sajana can barely apprehend what that sight means to her.

Sajana gradually wakes up to her senses at Croydon hospital. She tries to recall how she made her way to the hospital, but she can hardly remember. Instead, she finds a note tucked in an envelope beside her bed. After going through the note, her whole world turns upside down.

"Mum, if you are reading this, you are probably back in your senses. I'm sure you will be fine. But don't bother looking for me now. I love you, Mum, but knowingly or unknowingly, the death of my dad is forever linked to you. I could have saved my father as he left this world calling me over and over again. Had you not snatched my mobile phone yesterday, my dad would have been alive today. You keep saying that doubts invite destruction. You're probably right!"

How easy it is for Lily to write a note and leave her mother behind. She raised Lily as a single mother from the age of five until fifteen but yes, it was her fault to take hold of Lily's phone and not pick up Bryan's call. She would have probably picked up the call had Lily saved the contact's name, but Sajana didn't find it worthy enough to take a call from an unknown number at that hour of the night.

On one hand, Sajana is aggrieved by Bryan's death. She had spent six years of her life as his wife, but his drug addiction and frequent detention made both their lives slowly fall apart. When things got out of hand, they ended their relationship in divorce, and she tried her best to keep Lily away from him. But somewhere deep inside, she still loved him. She didn't know much about his whereabouts except that he got married twice after their divorce. She was completely ignorant about the fact that Lily and Bryan were in contact behind her back. Bryan's death has put an end to her past; however, her daughter's abscondment has drowned her present into a whirlpool of uncertainty.

***

Unspoken Desire

The joyful sounds of wedding music drifts over from the neighbouring house. Amita gazes through the window, observing the gathering crowd for Roma's wedding in her courtyard. She closes her eyes, lets out a deep sigh, and sobs softly before shutting the window. After composing herself, she opens it once again.

Roma sits in a car adorned with wedding decorations, and as the music starts playing, the car begins to move. Amita continues to watch until both the car and the music fade away. A sense of emptiness fills her room, prompting her to shut the door and window, where she surrenders to bitter tears.

Eventually, she wipes them away and experiences a fleeting moment of tranquillity. Just then, Nisha's voice startles her, calling her name, and she proceeds to open the door, wiping off the tears.

"Why are you crying, Didi[4]?" Nisha asks.

"Just because, I felt like crying," Amita replies honestly.

---

[4] *Elder sister*

"Aunty!" Riki's voice interjects, filling Amita with joy. She lifts Riki into her arms, planting kisses on her cheek, and cradles her niece in her lap.

"Oh, let go of me... my dress is creased now..." Riki playfully complains.

"Goodness, you and your antics!" Nisha laughs, joining Amita's side.

"You know how your brother-in-law is! I'm busy with work on other days, and he doesn't let me go anywhere on weekends," Nisha chuckles.

"Ugh! Do you really have to wait for weekends to come to your sister's place? Why don't you stay over? It's much closer to your workplace," Amita suggests.

"Well, it's not that simple! You'll understand once you get married," Nisha replies.

"Marriage? My marriage?" Amita ponders silently, her eyes welling up. Meanwhile, the sound of a motorcycle approaches. Nisha peeks out the window, grabs Riki's hand, and says, "Amita Didi, we're going to the temple and will be right back, okay? We won't be long. It's his birthday today, so we thought of paying a visit to the temple."

"Now I know your true motives for coming here, you little liar!" Amita playfully taunts her sister.

"We'll drop by when we return. Come on, Riki!" Nisha grabs Riki's hand, signalling her to join them, but Riki hesitates.

"Never mind, I'll stay here until you get back," Riki says.

"That's even better! Just make sure not to bother her too much." Nisha hurries downstairs, and Avinash starts the motorcycle. Amita watches them from her window, feeling a tinge of emptiness in her life. She turns around and hugs Riki.

"Aunty, can I stay with you during my summer vacation?" Riki asks in an affectionate and childish tone.

"Why only during the summer vacation, my dear? You can stay here for a lifetime." Amita pauses for a moment, directing her request to Riki. "But… you'll have to call me 'Mummy' instead of 'Aunty'.' Is that okay?"

"Yes, for sure." Riki smiles. Amita gazes at Riki intently.

"Mummy!" effortlessly echoes from Riki's lips as she calls out to Amita, the simplicity in her aunt's insistence making it a natural and easy expression for the child. Yearning to become a mother, Amita feels a poignant mix of joy and longing as her niece affectionately calls her 'Mummy'.'

"Riki!" Amita embraces Riki tightly, tears streaming down her face. Riki is unaware of the reason behind Amita's behaviour. Amita, however, feels sorry for Riki seeing her tears go unnoticed.

"I'll go outside and play," Riki runs off.

"Truly! If I were married, I would also have an eight- or nine-year-old daughter like Riki," Amita sighs deeply.

Amita's state of mind is peculiar. She is now thirty years old. Over the past ten to twelve years, she has attended numerous weddings of her school and college friends, yet she herself hasn't found that fortune. It's not that she lacks the desire to be adorned with various pieces of jewellery and bid farewell to her childhood home, enveloped in the joyous sounds of wedding music, to settle down in her husband's abode. However, fate has played a cruel trick on her. It's not that marriage proposals haven't come her way. After seeing her photo, people are generally eager to tie the knot, but nowadays, the situation necessitates interviews before marriage. And during these meetings, the other party often hesitates to proceed after seeing her in person.

After witnessing Roma's wedding, the same anxiety has resurfaced. "How long should I remain in my parents' home? How will my future sister-in-law tolerate my presence in this house once my younger brother gets married? Which parents wouldn't feel saddened by their grown-up daughter remaining unmarried?" Amita is consumed by such thoughts.

While Roma, the twenty-seven-year-old daughter of a millionaire, managed to get married despite her physical disabilities, Amita, with a perfectly healthy body, was cursed with a height of only four feet. Perhaps, if she were also the daughter of a millionaire, she would have already been married and had a couple of children running around.

***

Three months after Roma's marriage, she returns to her parents' home and visits Amita one day.

"Amita, you know what? Fate hasn't favoured us in the slightest. You're short, and I struggle with walking. Umesh only married me because of my millionaire father's wealth. The dowry, including 4 aana[5] of land, a car, a television set, and more, all ended up in the possession of his first wife, who now lives a lavish lifestyle," Roma shares in a dejected tone.

"First wife?"

"Yes, Amita… That woman convinced Umesh to marry me. They had a love marriage. Umesh's father had refused to let her into their house because she belonged to a lower caste. Only after Umesh lied to his father, claiming he had severed ties with that girl, that he was allowed in. And that's how we got married."

"Goodness! What kind of person is this man?" Amita responds in disbelief.

"Umesh often hurls profanities at me. He feels ashamed to introduce me, a disabled woman, as his wife. I have no desire to live, Amita… do you understand? No desire at all… It's better to die unmarried than enter such a disgraceful marriage," Roma confides.

After much contemplation, Amita finally concludes that she would not get married—not even if the other party desired it henceforth.

"Marriage is not the sole accomplishment in life. You can live on your own," Amita reassures herself. The sound of

[5] *A land area of 31.8 sq. metres*

wedding music resonates from another neighbour's house. Amita closes her window, plays her own music loudly, and reflects on Roma's words.

"Do you understand? It's better to die unmarried than enter such a disgraceful marriage."

***

Emily: My Neighbour

Despite wearing light makeup, her charm was on par with that of any beautiful actress. Babina was aware of her tall stature, fair complexion, beautiful large eyes, sweet gentle smile, and graceful personality—the only details she knew about Emily, her charming neighbour. Although she lived just a block away from Babina, their connection was merely one of proximity. In bustling London, who had the luxury of time for lengthy conversations? Their interactions were limited to occasional smiles exchanged while crossing paths.

As usual, Emily wore her five-inch-high heels and settled into the driver's seat of her red Nissan car. And as she reversed, the car swiftly zoomed away, disrupting the tranquillity of the night. It was a familiar sight for Babina to catch glimpses of Emily driving off in the dark. Emily's night time excursions were not uncommon, often starting around 2 a.m. in the morning. Throughout the weekdays, Emily's car would defy the tranquil darkness of the night, while on weekends, it would peacefully rest parked outside her house.

Babina whispered to herself, "How does she manage to drive in high heels? Maybe she keeps a spare pair of flats in her car." Numerous questions swirled in her mind, yet she never voiced them to anyone. Lost in her thoughts, she immersed herself in a world of imagination.

Avinash's voice broke her train of thought as he grumbled, "Please close the blinds. The outside lights are disturbing my sleep." Startled, Babina hastily shut the blinds and pulled the quilt over herself. She scooted closer to Avinash, seeking an embrace, but received no response, leaving her feeling disheartened.

"Why do you keep prying into other people's business so much? Even at 2 a.m., your snooping doesn't cease," Avinash grouched, rolling over and drifting back to sleep. Babina chose to remain silent in response. Once Emily's car had departed, shattering the silence of the night, the room fell back into quietude. Only the faint sound of Avinash's breathing could be heard.

Sleep eluded Babina for a while. Nights like this were not uncommon for her, yet she was unperturbed. She knew she had ample time during the day to catch up on her sleep. After Avinash left for work, Babina had little to occupy her time. Aside from tending to household chores and preparing meals for the two of them, her schedule was quite empty. Those close to her, including family and friends, considered Babina fortunate.

"Even in a city like London, you're living the life of a housewife. You must be having the time of your life!" Many people would comment, but Babina hadn't fully understood the implications of those words.

"Well, perhaps they're right. I don't have to stress about finding a job or dealing with the hustle outside the house. But does that truly make me fortunate?" Babina pondered; her gaze fixated on the dimly flickering lightbulb in the dark room. She drew a parallel between herself and the lightbulb, and let out a deep sigh.

Motivated by numerous desires, aspirations, and dreams, Babina entered into marriage with Avinash. She had embarked on pursuing a law degree after completing high school at a government school in Biratnagar[6]. Babina couldn't simply let go of her bright future, filled with hopes of furthering her education in the United Kingdom. Consequently, she blindly accepted the marriage proposal from her maternal aunt. At the tender age of nineteen, she tied the knot with Avinash and relocated to London, driven by her ambition to become a lawyer abroad.

Babina cherished her lofty dreams, but she understood that in reality, dreams often remain mere fantasies. Not all dreams come true. She would somehow console herself with this notion, silently burying her own stories of personal failures. Perhaps she saw no alternative but to do so, considering herself fortunate to have found a sincere and gentle partner like Avinash.

Somehow, Babina managed to start her law studies in London—thanks to Avinash's promise to enrol her in a law college. However, she struggled to cope with the challenges posed by the education system in the UK.

---

[6] *Biratnagar lies in the eastern part of Nepal, serving as a significant industrial and commercial centre in the region.*

Coming from a Nepali-medium school, the transition to an English-medium college proved to be an uphill battle. Babina found herself engulfed in a sea of worries, sinking deeper into the abyss of despair, rendering her unable to stay afloat.

This relentless state took a severe toll on her health. She found herself constantly immersed in rumination, trapped in a cycle of thoughts that consumed her daily life. Despite her efforts, she couldn't extricate herself from the whirlpool of overthinking. Avinash, being a doctor, made valiant attempts to rescue her from this predicament. Unfortunately, his professional expertise could only do so much to restore her failing health.

***

Five months had elapsed since Emily became their neighbour, yet Babina hadn't found an opportunity to truly connect with her and engage in a meaningful conversation. Whenever she cooked Nepali dishes like momo[7] and selroti[8], Babina felt the desire to share them with Emily. However, she hesitated, wondering if Emily would appreciate Nepalese cuisine. Undeniably, Emily's arrival had brought about changes in Babina. Her appearance, complexion, and liveliness ignited a newfound enthusiasm within Babina's heart. Babina, who had previously lost interest in wearing makeup, now yearned to enhance her

---

[7] A steamed or fried dumpling, typical of South Asian cuisine, popular in Nepal.

[8] A ring-shaped traditional rice bread/doughnut, popular in Nepal.

beauty. She found herself reaching for lipstick and powder, and frequently gazed at her reflection in the mirror throughout the day.

Like every other night, the sound of Emily's car disrupted the peacefulness of the neighbourhood. Avinash, peacefully asleep, remained unfazed by the noise. In contrast, Babina's curiosity prompted her to wake up and discreetly observe Emily. As she peered out the window, Babina couldn't help but admire Emily's charming personality. The softly illuminated streetlights in the serene night seemed to enhance Emily's allure even further.

"Babina, please go to sleep. How much longer will you stay awake like this? While you have no obligations, remember that I have work tomorrow," Avinash grumbled, attempting to return to his slumber. Startled by Avinash's comment, Babina once again felt the sting of her own shortcomings and failures.

"Really, what work do I have? Compared to the struggles faced by other women in this country, it amounts to nothing. Absolutely nothing!" Babina thought, tears welling up in her eyes. However, there was no one around to witness her silent pain. Avinash was her entire world, but she couldn't comprehend what Avinash's world truly entailed.

Despite adorning herself for the past couple of days, hoping to capture his attention when he returned from work, Babina discovered that Avinash showed no interest in her at all. It seemed as though her efforts to dress up and wear makeup had no effect on Avinash, leaving her without any response from him. She increased her endeavours in cooking and trying out new recipes for him, yet there was a lack of acknowledgment.

Babina reminisced about the excitement of their first two years of marriage, but now everything felt meaningless. Not only through her cuisines and makeup, but also through the sleepless nights she experienced, Babina inferred that Avinash had distanced himself from her. Her eyes wandered restlessly, longing for Avinash's touch. Avinash's constant excuses of tiredness and work obligations made it clear to Babina that she had lost his intimacy. Babina contemplated how Avinash, who shared the same bed, had gradually slipped away from her. This night, like every other night, sleep evaded her.

Sleepless nights and uneventful days became Babina's constant companions. She lacked someone special to confide in. Avinash's Nepali friends were scattered about an hour's drive away. During gatherings or dinner nights, Babina found herself bonding with the wives of Avinash's friends. However, those connections were limited to those specific gatherings. Babina would leave with promises of keeping in touch, occasionally making phone calls, but never receiving any in return. She hesitated, fearing that her calls might be seen as a nuisance.

Nonetheless, during these infrequent gatherings that occurred every two or three months, Babina would find solace in hearty laughter and conversations in Nepali. Avinash also seemed more at ease during these events. However, Babina particularly noticed that Avinash appeared closer to Prema than to her on such occasions. It seemed that there were more pictures of Avinash and Prema embracing and posing together than pictures of Avinash with Babina in his camera.

Prema, who had been living in London for fifteen years, was the wife of Avinash's school friend Amar. She unabashedly clung to Avinash's company without hesitation. Although Avinash seemed to welcome Prema's flirtatious advances, Babina lacked the courage to address her concerns. She feared being labelled as conservative because, during her five-year stay in England, it was common to see couples taking casual pictures with each other's spouses.

At times, Babina felt that if her relationship with Avinash were at least as close as the one between Avinash and Prema, she would consider her married life a success. Not only at night, but even during the day, love and affection from Avinash felt like a distant reality.

Babina relied on Avinash's love as her sole pillar of support in life. Her dream of becoming a lawyer gradually faded away due to the physical weakness brought on by her illness. In the early days of their life in England, when Avinash's friends inquired about Babina's occupation, he took great pride and delight in proclaiming, "Well, she's studying to become a lawyer! She'll be a lawyer in a few years!"

However, as time went on, Babina's journey took a different course. Unfortunately, it wasn't a favourable one. Her aspirations of becoming a lawyer remained confined to the realm of dreams. Instead, she became known simply as 'sister-in-law' among Avinash's friends. Even back in Biratnagar, her identity was tied to being a 'Mrs. Doctor'.' People in the neighbourhood would address her by that name after her marriage to Avinash. Babina had become the wife of a doctor, yet her own body suffered from an invisible ailment that no doctor could diagnose.

Babina's illness was strange, to say the least. It caused her headaches when she tried to turn the pages of a book, made her tremble at the slightest hint of stress, and plunged her into deeper thoughts when she contemplated things. While she had heard of depression on occasion, she had limited knowledge about it. She attempted medication for her illness, but it seemed to bring more adverse effects than benefits. Consequently, she grew weary of it and resigned herself to the mercy of time and fate.

***

Since early morning, a light drizzle had been falling. Babina's attention was caught by a loud noise accompanied by the heavy rainfall. She opened her door and stepped outside, noticing a fallen signboard. Babina hadn't realised when her neighbour Emily's board had been placed in front of her house. She made an effort to lift it and put it back in place, but the strong wind made it difficult for the board to stay upright.

Suddenly, her eyes fell on the letters written on the board and she was quite startled. It dawned on her that Emily's house was up for sale. A profound sense of sadness washed over Babina upon this realisation. Emily had brought some small moments of joy into her life, and even her occasional smiles had brought Babina a sense of happiness. It seemed that this connection with Emily wouldn't last much longer.

Babina had found joy in observing Emily's activities, from the colour of her lipstick and her high-heeled shoes to the purse she carried. Emily's entire persona was endearing to Babina. Inspired by Emily, Babina had recently started taking better care of her own appearance. She also yearned to learn how to drive, just like Emily, but lacked the courage to sign up for driving classes. Babina had attempted to discuss this with Avinash, seeking permission and hoping for encouragement, but she couldn't bring herself to do so.

Over the past five years, she had lost many things, including her confidence to express herself. She no longer liked anything about herself, only admiring everything about Emily. This was why she worried about feeling lonely after Emily's departure. Babina reminded herself that nothing in life was permanent. After all, Emily was just a neighbour. With this thought in mind, Babina gathered her strength and composed herself.

***

The city of London, plagued by constant rainfall, echoed with anguish. Within the desolate walls of their house, a profound sense of despair filled the air. A document lay on the table, pleading for a signature, symbolising the impending turmoil. Babina found herself unable to shed tears or mourn the situation. She was plagued by confusion, unable to comprehend where, when, and how things had gone wrong.

She had left no stone unturned in fulfilling her duties as a devoted wife. It wasn't her fault that she couldn't conceive children. It wasn't her choice to abandon her studies, and she couldn't bear the sole responsibility of maintaining the same level of excitement in their relationship as they had in the early days of their marriage. As she stared at the words written on the document, she began to dissect her perceived mistakes. Her emotions overwhelmed her, leading to tears, screams, and desperate pleas directed at Avinash.

"Please, Avinash, don't abandon me! How can I face my parents? Where do I turn to? In this foreign land, you are the only one I have to call my own."

Avinash stood motionless, resembling a lifeless statue. His eyes lacked any trace of affection or compassion for Babina. Firm in his decision, he hadn't consulted or spoken a word to her. The sudden appearance of the divorce papers felt like a random act of terrorism, making it difficult for her to believe. Although their relationship and household had lost its spark and tenderness, Babina had accepted their situation and the constraints it imposed. At least she wasn't a subject of mockery or sympathy in that regard. She had been willing to sacrifice anything for Avinash if the need arose.

However, today his demand called for the sacrifice of her very existence. Time was testing the strength of her love, and she couldn't let her emotions falter this time. Despite

Avinash's lack of love, affection, and touch, she hadn't allowed it to disrupt their relationship.

In a fit of anger triggered by the divorce papers, Babina impulsively threw a wok out the window. It was evening, and as usual, Emily's car was parked outside her house. Babina's anger didn't fear the consequences this time—not of her neighbours, society, or even the police. Consequently, the wok smashed Emily's car windshield, landing in the middle of the road with a loud crash.

Startled by the sound, Emily rushed out of her house to see what had happened. For the first time, Babina saw Emily's face up close, feeling nervous in that moment. She couldn't contain her personal anger within the confines of her house. While her eyes were filled with fury at the divorce papers Avinash had presented, her heart was heavy with regret for the damage to Emily's car.

Contrary to Babina's expectations, Emily approached her and embraced her. In this unfamiliar city, receiving someone's affection had been limited to her imagination. Babina felt deeply ashamed of her actions. If it had been any other neighbours, they would have likely called the police by now.

"I am deeply sorry! Please, don't involve the police. I will have your car repaired today. I promise you, this will never happen again," Babina apologised, filled with gratitude for Emily's kindness and support.

"Everyone makes mistakes. Please forgive me for mine. I didn't intend to come between you two, but I failed." Babina remained embraced by Emily.

She couldn't understand who had come between whom. At that moment, Avinash stepped forward.

"Babina, please forgive me. I had intended to tell you the truth, but I didn't want to hurt you by confessing that I am leaving you for someone else," Avinash said, placing his hand on Babina's shoulder. However, his touch had no impact on Babina today. Despite yearning for Avinash's love and affection for years, his touch now held no meaning to her. Babina felt like a mere body, devoid of any emotional connection.

In the midst of this, Babina spoke, "Who is this 'someone else'?" She looked at both of their faces, but received no response. Babina had her answer.

"In the end, you have left me, Avinash, regardless of why or for whom," Babina's eyes welled up with tears, but she managed to hold them back. She steeled her heart and quickly signed the paper that he had brought.

Throughout this exchange, Emily remained silent and eventually retreated to her own house.

Babina's house was enveloped in a haunting silence. While Avinash had achieved the freedom he desired by ending his marriage with Babina, she was left utterly shattered. Babina had never regarded Avinash with suspicion or felt the need to do so. However, she couldn't hold Avinash bound by the thread of her love.

It was only recently that she discovered Emily, who left for work at 2 a.m., and Avinash, who departed at 6 a.m., both worked at the same hospital. She had never even fathomed the possibility that Doctor Avinash and Nurse Emily would become involved so quickly. Avinash had never disclosed this to her, nor had she noticed any signs from Emily, whom she had admired greatly. She now felt like a stranger in her own home, clueless about when her life and dreams had been stolen away from her.

Babina's self-confidence had suffered a severe blow. It seemed that her vulnerability stemmed from her inability to balance her family and personal growth simultaneously. As a result, she had resigned herself to seeing her existence as a mere compromise, a trial she had to endure.

Avinash's words lingered in her mind, "After the divorce, you can still live in this house." By that time, the "For Sale" signboard that had been outside Emily's house had disappeared. Perhaps Avinash lacked the courage to move next door to Emily or to bring her into the same house. However, Emily had made the decision to sell her house and settle a few miles away, closer to the hospital—a fact that Babina discovered only when Avinash revealed his intention to leave their house. With promises from Avinash to take care of her financial responsibilities and household needs, he departed with Emily. Babina felt like a mere spectator in the unfolding events, caught in a whirlwind of emotions and uncertainty.

Babina found herself in a state of loneliness, both in her mind and in her physical surroundings. Her mind was devoid of companionship, just like her body, her bed, and the desolate room she occupied. Gone were the days when Babina would glance out of her window at 2 a.m., or when she would hear Avinash's irritated voice asking her to close the blinds, disturbed by the outside lights.

Now, she stood at a crossroads between living and dying, grappling with the overwhelming turmoil within, unsure of how to find solace or inner peace.

***

Harimaya's Daughter-In-Law

"What's all this fuss about the caste system[9] even in today's age?" After Harimaya's son married an American girl, rumours began to circulate in the neighbourhood. People were surprised and curious, asking, "Is that Harimaya's son?" This unexpected development caught Nili off guard. Although Nili and Harimaya were not same-age buddies, they would spend their days gossiping and talking negatively about others.

In the beginning, Nili was surprised by Harimaya's knack for backbiting and meddling in others' affairs, but as their bond grew, Nili couldn't help but be influenced by Harimaya's charismatic effect, despite their twenty-five-year age difference. These women, whose lives revolved around household chores, found pleasure in spreading rumours and talking behind people's backs. That's why the neighbours tended to avoid them, especially after gossip about Kapila spread in the locality.

---

[9] *The caste system in Nepal, deeply ingrained in its social fabric, categorises individuals into distinct groups, influencing societal roles and interactions. Despite ongoing efforts to address inequality, it remains a significant aspect shaping relationships and opportunities in Nepalese culture.*

One day, when Kapila, a fourteen-year-old girl, embarked on a trip to visit her best friend in West Nepal, people saw Harka Bahadur boarding the same bus. The gossip queens seized this opportunity and spread rumours that Kapila had eloped with Harka Bahadur. Kapila returned home because she forgot her bus ticket. When she heard about the rumour, she was shocked and disturbed. In frustration, she cancelled her plans to visit her friend. Since that day, all the residents of the locality have been cautious around Harimaya.

Indeed, Harimaya's son married his love, Julie. However, their love story was only a year old, with Julie coming all the way from America. Harimaya pleaded with her son not to marry Julie for the sake of their social reputation. But when her son informed her that Julie was already pregnant with their child and he couldn't abandon her, Harimaya was devastated. After all, he was her only child and companion in her old age.

What else could poor Harimaya do? So, she steeled her heart and prepared for a grand wedding. Harimaya's son and Julie tied the knot amidst great celebration. Many residents, including Nili, attended the extravagant occasion.

With Harimaya's American daughter-in-law, came an abundance of wealth. The modest wooden chairs in Harimaya's home were quickly replaced with high-class sofas. The old hand-knitted rugs in the living room were substituted with expensive velvety carpets. The sound of bells chiming from Harimaya's home early in the morning gradually ceased. These sounds, which disturbed the neighbours' sleep, were usually Harimaya reciting hymns and bhajans.

Among the residents in Harimaya's neighbourhood was Shiva Ram Purohit[10]'s daughter, who played Western music until midnight, disturbing the sleep of others. Nili's house was located between Shiva Ram Purohit's house and Harimaya's house, so her family had to use cotton buds in their ears to get a good night's sleep. Sometimes, the cotton buds would fall out during the night, causing them to occasionally miss Harimaya's morning rituals but never the sound of Western music.

Harimaya was a deeply religious person and devoted herself to worship and prayers with great enthusiasm. Whenever she went to the temple, she would bring flowers and offerings for Nili as well. They would engage in various discussions and stories about gods. Sometimes, if Harimaya had a Satyanarayan Pooja[11] at home, she would insist and persuade Nili to observe the fasts. Whether knowingly or unknowingly, Nili also became adept at observing fasts. Even though Nili wasn't skilled in remembering or performing the worship rituals, in recent times, she had developed an uncanny interest towards Harimaya's religious activities.

Harimaya was an old woman, but not too old. She was more religious than Nili, who initially didn't believe much in idol worship. However, Harimaya inspired her to become more religious, and eventually, she embraced

---

[10] *A Hindu priest*
[11] *A religious ritual worship of the Hindu god Vishnu.*

religious practices. Like Harimaya, Nili started observing Ekadashi[12] and Purnima[13] fasts without fail.

Although Nili initially knew little about palmistry, Harimaya's continuous insistence and teachings made her quite knowledgeable in reading palms. As a result, Nili felt she was no less than the row of astrologers at Tundikhel[14] who read people's futures. She could somewhat accurately match everyone's past and future. When her friends and relatives gathered around her to have their palms read by Nili, she felt like a great astrologer and was grateful to Harimaya for imparting this skill to her.

Initially, Nili had little to do on a daily basis other than performing household chores, sending her children to school, and spending the day either sleeping or knitting. As she grew tired of idling around, she started visiting Harimaya's house to alleviate her boredom. During those visits, her days mostly revolved around hearing the petty gossip that Harimaya shared about the residents of the locality, such as which daughter had eloped with whom, which son had married whom, who sold their house, who bought it, whose house was mortgaged for a loan, and so on. But as life goes, what goes around comes around.

---

[12] A sacred day observed by doing a fast on every 11th tithi (lunar day) of the lunar month as per the Hindu calendar.

[13] A full Moon or new Moon Day and is considered auspicious for fasting.

[14] Astrologers at Tundikhel, a historic open ground in Kathmandu, Nepal, often gather to offer insights into the future based on ancient astrological practices.

Those who speak ill of others will eventually face the same themselves—it's karma.

Harimaya had talked extensively behind their backs when Jiten had an intercaste marriage, tying the knot with a Brahmin[15] girl. Harimaya had spared no effort in backbiting about Jiten, saying, "Couldn't he find a Newari[16] girl in the whole world? He had to marry a Brahmin, that blind fool!" Now that her own son had married an American girl, Harimaya was left speechless.

Fearful of being caught or questioned abruptly, Harimaya stopped coming out to their usual spot on the terrace to gossip with Nili. When Nili was recently married, she used to wear Kurta-Salwar[17]. Harimaya's outdated belief that married women should strictly wear a saree had led her to rebel against Nili's choice of clothing.

Just a few days ago, Julie was seen jogging in shorts. It was nothing new for Julie, but in their narrow-minded society, Harimaya's daughter-in-law appeared extremely modern. Poor Harimaya! She used to tell people that she would make her future daughter-in-law massage her feet and do as she pleased. Perhaps Harimaya's mother-in-law had treated her the same way, and as an act of revenge, she wanted the same from her daughter-in-law. Unfortunately,

---

[15] The Nepalese Brahmin, considered as high caste and rooted in priestly and scholarly traditions, is witnessing evolving roles and perspectives in the changing cultural and religious landscape.

[16] Of Newar caste, a community considered as the historical inhabitants of Kathmandu valley.

[17] A traditional combination dress worn by women in South Asia.

Harimaya's dream of making her daughter-in-law dance to her tune was unsuccessful.

Sometimes, when Julie had back pain during workouts, Harimaya was seen massaging her back, as suggested by her son. Witnessing this, Nili couldn't help but silently mock the situation. Harimaya's face turned red with embarrassment, and she closed the curtains. It had been more than a week since the curtains were last opened. Nili started hoping that one day the curtains would open, giving the neighbours a glimpse into Harimaya's life. As a result, Nili's routine of going out on the terrace increased even more.

***

Citizenship

It was the last day of November. The scorching heat had stirred up the roads, seeking relief from one another. However, the weather in Melbourne seemed to mock them, intensifying its heat as if flaunting its might. Meanwhile, the train glided swiftly at its own pace, unaffected by the road's struggle with the weather. The roads sensed the train taunting them from a distance, wishing they could race alongside it to enjoy the refreshing breeze it created. Yet, they remained silent and still as always.

As I sat inside the train, numerous roads passed by, and I found myself contemplating their state of mind. Time slipped away unnoticed, and I failed to realise my intended stop. It wasn't until reaching the next station that I realised I had missed my destination. The allure of analysing the roads' mindset had consumed me to the point where I had inadvertently travelled well beyond Warrigal Road and Watsford Road.

How absent-minded I am! Once lost in thoughts, I often lose track of my surroundings. Today was no exception. I had been traveling the same route by train for years without being preoccupied with such thoughts. I was genuinely amazed by why these roads captured my attention today.

I made my way back to the station to catch another train, feeling frustrated by the oppressive heat that seemed to mock me. As I stood there, I observed the intersecting paths of Warrigal Road and Watsford Road stretching into the distance, serving the students who walked by—a scene I had witnessed countless times from the train. But amidst this familiar sight, the railway tracks silently shared their tale of hardship with those two roads. From the platform, I found myself immersed in analysing the bond between them.

I had prepared a list of household items to sell, which I still held in my hands. However, a sudden gust of wind, stirred up by a passing train, whisked the note from my hands and carried it to the far corner of the platform. I hurriedly searched and got hold of the list, too preoccupied to bid farewell to the roads. Silently promising to reunite with them later, I made my way into the college.

Inside the classrooms, an air of desolation lingered as the absence of students echoed throughout. With international students returning to their home countries, an unusual silence pervaded the surroundings. Yet, my mind brimmed with an extraordinary excitement, being in my final year. The longing to return to my own country consumed my thoughts, causing my mind to wander. With only a few days left, my mind was neither completely restrained nor entirely free. Perhaps that's why I found myself particularly drawn to these roads.

Stella emerged from a distance, gesturing towards the noticeboard as she inquired, "Are you here to post your list?" I responded with a smile. As she approached me, she empathetically remarked, "Being an international student can be quite challenging, right? Sometimes it's the hassle of acquiring things, and other times it's the struggle of selling them. We can't simply discard items either, considering the cost involved."

Stella proceeded to affix her own list onto the noticeboard. My spirits dampened as I glanced at the lengthy row of posts already hanging there. Not only Stella's, but a multitude of other posts vied for attention, striving to attract the interest of new students.

Not far from where I stood, a person scanned the noticeboard intently, clearly in search of something to buy. On a whim, I approached him and swiftly pinned my list right before his eyes. He looked at me, quickly noting down my contact details, expressing his interest in buying the TV and refrigerator. I felt a sense of relief wash over me. Amidst the sea of items being offered for sale, he somehow singled out mine—something that surprised me.

Overhearing our conversation, Stella approached me and remarked, "You lucky girl!" Her words, however, carried a subtle hint of envy. Envy was indeed a defining characteristic of Stella.

As our conversation progressed, I shared with the young man, who was interested in purchasing my items, that I would soon be returning to my home country of Nepal after completing my studies. I expressed my eagerness to sell off all my belongings at a reasonable price, hoping for a quick resolution. Upon hearing the name Nepal, he simply responded, "Oh, Nepal!"

Judging by his appearance, I could infer that he hailed from Malaysia, Indonesia, or Vietnam. However, without thinking, I blurted out, "Are you from China?" This question slipped out due to the significant presence of Chinese people in Australia. He informed me that he was a permanent resident of Australia but preferred not to disclose his country of origin. Sensing his hesitation, I deemed it appropriate not to probe further.

Throughout my two years of experience, I encountered very few individuals who were familiar with Nepal. Despite this, I was convinced that this person at least had some understanding of my country. However, while traveling abroad, I discovered that the belief recognising Nepal as the home of Mount Everest, the world's highest peak, was often a misconception. While it was true that almost everyone knew about Mount Everest, when I mentioned that I was from the land of Mount Everest, they would often assume I was from either India or China.

Each time this happened, it would crush a small part of my Nepali heart, leaving me feeling squeezed between two imposing boulders. A mixture of humiliation and frustration would well up inside me, and I would passionately exclaim, "Mount Everest is in Nepal, not India or China." Yet, I wasn't sure if my outbursts had any impact on their understanding. The daily encounters of such ignorance gradually wore down my ability to cope with these situations.

With my heart wounded by these painful remarks, I would contemplate confronting them and posing some questions. However, I hesitated, wondering if these individuals who claimed to be familiar with Nepal truly knew that Mount Everest was located within its borders. Despite the internal conflict, I refrained from confronting them unnecessarily, choosing not to unleash the pent-up frustrations I had accumulated.

The cafeteria, once filled with bustling activity, now appeared desolate as fewer students occupied the space. I sat there, gazing at the forlorn tables and chairs, while reading a magazine. Suddenly, I was taken aback when I saw Sicily walking hand in hand with the guy who had promised to purchase my belongings earlier. It was no surprise that Sicily looked more conceited and flamboyant than before.

Originally from Russia, Sicily had moved to Australia with her parents at a young age and grew up here. It was in that very cafeteria where I first met her, but since my vacation began, I hadn't had a chance to see her again. This encounter marked the first time I had seen her since then.

Sicily's face lit up with excitement when she spotted me, and she promptly took a seat directly in front of me. Unable to contain my curiosity, I immediately asked her, "Did you visit Nepal?" To my surprise, she responded with confusion, "Nepal?" Her reaction left me astonished. She then left my side and approached the guy she had arrived with, inviting him to join us. Within moments, both were seated in front of me.

Continuing her conversation, Sicily enthusiastically shared, "Not only did I visit Nepal, but I also brought something back from there." She introduced the person beside her, saying, "This is Manish. He arrived just three days ago. I sent him here to gather the necessities to help him settle in smoothly. Once he's settled, we plan to get married in the next few days."

My astonishment grew as I observed Manish, a Nepali guy, and I found myself staring at him without any immediate reaction. His reserved demeanour made it evident that he had been an Australian citizen for only the past three days. Perhaps he felt awkward or ashamed about revealing his birthplace or the country he came from, which would explain why he hadn't disclosed his country of origin when I asked earlier. Moreover, it saddened me that despite our shared Nepali heritage, I couldn't elicit a sense of belonging or affection from him.

Sicily appeared very happy after meeting Manish. However, for Manish, it was a twofold accomplishment: Sicily and Australian citizenship. I didn't want to make Manish feel more embarrassed by asking him about Nepal. Without jeopardising his dream of becoming an Australian citizen, I bid farewell to Sicily, stealing a glance at his expressionless face for one last time.

The train was still 10 minutes away. I felt overwhelmed by the love that Warrigal Road and Watsford Road had shown me. It was as if they were urging me to wipe away their tears and sweat. Cars were harshly plying over them, but those roads, carrying years of love and friendship, seemed to beg me not to return. It felt like Warrigal Road and Watsford Road were thanking me for understanding their pain and shedding tears as they watched me from across the railway tracks.

I turned coldly and walked toward the train. The roads passed by one after another, but Ratnapark and Bhotahiti roads, bustling thoroughfares in the heart of Kathmandu, were nowhere to be found there.

***

Insignificant Letters

The letterbox in front of my house greets me with a gentle smile. In contrast to its previous mocking behaviour, today's peculiar smile attracts my attention. As I notice a couple of letters peeking out from its little window, I change my direction and head towards the letterbox. However, I can't help but feel a bit apprehensive, hoping it won't ridicule my steps towards it.

It surprises me how much affection I have developed for this letterbox since I moved to Melbourne. During the first few weeks after my arrival, the letterbox used to summon me numerous times a day. But today, after many days, I find a mixture of affection towards me in its smile, and it compels me to open its door.

Inside, I find four or five letters as usual. However, as I see the letters addressed to my housemate, it plunges me back into the familiar sea of pain. Just then, Sushila rushes outside, shouting, "Are those my letters?" All I can offer in response is a smile. I don't feel like burdening those cheerful letters addressed to her with my bitter experiences.

Clutching the four letters tightly, Sushila rushes towards her room, oblivious to the tears welling up in my eyes. She slams the door shut behind her. I collapse onto the bed, overwhelmed by the desire to unleash a torrent of tears onto my pillow. The tears escape from the corners of my eyes, tracing a path down my cheeks.

As someone knocks on the door, my anguish remains unaddressed. A voice from outside calls, "Nisha, look, there's a letter from Ritesh. He was asking about you too. He even sent a photo. Please open the door."

Taking a deep breath, I summon the strength to hold back the flood of tears. But they persist, refusing to be restrained. I don't want to dampen Sushila's happiness with my own tears. That's why I attempt to conceal my emotions and proceed to open the door.

Sushila enters the room and settles on the bed. I make a futile attempt to hide the tear-soaked pillow by draping my jacket over it. At the same time, Sushila tries to show me a photo by placing it on the same pillow, resulting in a playful struggle of who can place their items first. In the midst of this, Sushila notices the damp pillow and exclaims, "Are you crying? How did the pillow get wet?"

I quickly respond, "Oh, it's nothing. I just accidentally spilled some water while drinking." I keep my emotions locked inside me. Perhaps due to her own excitement, Sushila fails to observe the expression on my face.

As she reads the letter, she exclaims, "Look, Ritesh is coming here to study. Nisha, isn't that great news?" I nod my head in agreement, though I have no idea what she's asking me or what response she expects. After all, I am lost in my own world of thoughts.

The sound of something being dropped into the letterbox outside startles me, capturing my attention. Someone has slipped more mail through it. Filled with the same longing and aspirations, I approach the letterbox with the intention of opening it. As I peer inside, one particular letter immediately grabs my attention, causing my tears to transform into sheer joy.

With both hands, I cradle the letter against my chest. Finally, there's a post addressed to me. This discovery fills me with happiness. Previously, my happiness had been dampened by the absence of any letter bearing my name. Today, I anticipate that the joyful news contained within this letter will soothe all the tears I have shed so far. With this hopeful thought in mind, I examine the sender's name on the envelope. To my surprise, it bears a foreign name I have never encountered before.

I decide to open the letter right there, outside, to satisfy my curiosity. "If you fail to pay your telephone bill on time, your line will be disconnected in two days," it reads. In a hurry, I rush towards the door, calling out Sushila's name. Just then, the phone begins to ring. Considering I don't know many people in this foreign land who would call me, my hopes rise with each ring.

"Could it be someone from the telecom company?" I wonder as I hurry inside the house. However, I remain composed as I prepare to answer the call. If Sushila can receive four letters in one day, perhaps a phone call awaits me as well. Setting aside my hopes from the letterbox, I reach out to pick up the receiver. To my dismay, Sushila has already picked up the phone.

For a brief moment, I am left speechless. I cannot forcefully take the receiver from Sushila's grasp. However, a sense of disappointment washes over me as I realise how Sushila tends to intervene in every aspect of my life.

"Hey, Ritesh! I received your letter today. When are you planning to come here?" She bombards the person on the other end of the line with questions. My steps become heavy with helplessness, and the hopes in my heart start to wither away. It seems that even my tears are weary of flowing, as they show no signs of trickling down any longer.

In the evening, I notice the letterbox once again, smiling at me from outside my window. Unconsciously, my eyes scan its small window and come to a halt. Another post appears to be peeking out from it. However, I can hardly muster the strength to go and receive it.

***

Growing Civilisation

"What is this life? Merely a speck of dust in the face of death, and yet we witness terrible acts like arson, envy, murder, and rape every day. It's a harsh reality that death is inevitable, but people still can't let go of their insatiable desire for money." Pranita brought up the topic of life during our conversation.

Normally, we discussed different events and issues in society, but today Pranita seemed more serious than ever before. Wanting to keep the discussion going, I added, "It seems that the world now revolves around three W's: Wealth, Women, and Wine. The true essence of civilisation has been abandoned, reducing women to mere objects of pleasure, and blurring the boundaries of profanity in the pursuit of wealth. Day by day, addiction continues to rise."

Just as I finished speaking, Praveen rushed in, breathless, to deliver devastating news: "Rama, did you hear? Aakash had a terrible accident at Baneshwor and died on the spot." I was momentarily stunned, unable to fathom Aakash's sudden demise. Road accidents have been so common in Kathmandu and roads are not safe at all, especially for bikers. Vivid scenes of accidents flashed before my eyes. "Aakash is dead? It can't be!" I cried out. While I still possessed the ability to process and react to such situations, Pranita collapsed right then and there, her body giving way without a word.

Fear consumed me, worried that Pranita might meet the same tragic fate as Aakash on the very same day. Without wasting a moment, Praveen and I rushed Pranita to Bir hospital. After what felt like an eternity, Pranita regained consciousness, but the anguish and sorrow etched on her face were deeply distressing. In the adjacent room lay Aakash's lifeless body, but we could hardly muster the courage to look at his face. According to reports, he had fallen off a bridge while riding his motorcycle.

"Where is Aakash?" Pranita exclaimed, struggling to rise from her position. She had only a faint inkling of the reality. After a brief moment, she composed herself. When I informed her that Aakash was in the next room, she rushed out, calling out his name. Pranita's voice reverberated through the hospital, echoing for the last time when she saw the lifeless body of Aakash. She never got another chance.

By the time we reached the room where Aakash lay, Pranita had already lost consciousness, and her unconsciousness would be eternal. Praveen carried Pranita's young daughter, who was too small to comprehend or mourn the loss of her parents. It was left to us to perform their final rites.

It had been two years since Aakash and Pranita got married. I had only recently discovered that prior to their marriage, Aakash had served a two-year prison sentence for involvement in illegal activities. Pranita had learned about it after their marriage, indirectly hinting at it on a couple of occasions, but she always carried the burden of her husband's misdeeds, fearing society's judgment.

I realised that Aakash would come home intoxicated every day, which bothered Pranita and prompted her to confide in me. Initially, I didn't probe further, assuming that many husbands in our society returned home in a similar state. However, I eventually discovered the truth.

Pranita had mentioned that Aakash wasn't feeling well and had gone for a blood test. The results revealed that he was HIV/AIDS positive. Perhaps unable to comprehend the purpose of life, he might have jumped off the bridge. Alternatively, his tragic accident could have been a result of his disturbed mental condition. By that time, Pranita may have also been infected with AIDS. We couldn't help but wonder if their daughter had also contracted the virus. Filled with uncertainty, we had her blood tested, and thankfully, by God's grace, Pranita's daughter was safe and healthy.

Poor girl, Pranita displayed remarkable resilience and patience. She never complained to me about her husband's wrongdoing and addiction. Aakash would often be absent from home for many nights. I would notice it when Pranita sat by the window late at night, gazing outside. When I asked her about it in the morning, she would make unsuccessful attempts to lie, attributing her presence at the window to the heat. I happened to see her because I stayed awake studying for my exams until midnight. There were likely countless nights when Aakash didn't come home.

We assumed the responsibility of caring for Pranita's daughter. Pranita often mentioned that she had few relatives, if any. While I had no objections to raising her as a friend or neighbour's child, I worried about the girl's future. How would she react when she grew older and learned about her father's misdeeds? How much resentment would she hold toward him? Aakash, who always portrayed himself as civilised and gentle, tragically passed away and in doing so, made his daughter an orphan, taking the life of his own wife.

Indeed! Civilisation is often defined by some as the freedom to do whatever they please. Unfortunately, Akash seemed to have forgotten that his primary duty was to bring complete happiness to his spouse. His addiction to prostitution, like many others, contributed to the coarseness of our society. Akash squandered the money he earned on such immoral activities, and it wasn't until after his demise that rumours began circulating in the neighbourhood, revealing the truth. Perhaps that explains why Pranita's wedding ornaments and jewellery mysteriously disappeared day by day.

"These days, the news headlines in Nepal often discuss the legalisation and open acceptance of prostitution in certain areas as a means to protect our girls from rape. They argue that people should have the freedom to do anything according to their choice. It's not surprising that this version of civilisation is leading to the downfall of human society," remarked Praveen, seated across from me.

Although Praveen and I seldom debated such topics, his words instantly reminded me of Pranita, with whom I would occasionally engage in heated discussions. Eager to share my perspective, I quickly responded, "The concept of civilisation encompasses a wide range of interpretations, often likened to a circle that emerges and eventually returns to its origin. In ancient times, scarcity led people to go unclothed, while today, some choose to wear less clothing. It's possible that someday we may witness a society where nudity becomes the ultimate expression of civilisation."

At that moment, we heard Pranita's daughter crying, and we rushed to attend to her.

***

Immigrant's Heart

I was constantly amazed by Maria's profound love and commitment to dogs. She could always be spotted walking her dog Drogo in the streets of London, whether it was morning, day, or evening. Apart from exchanging simple greetings like hi and hellos, we didn't share a special bond. I had recently moved to the neighbourhood, so our acquaintance was relatively new.

On some occasions, I caught myself unintentionally staring at her from behind when she walked ahead of me. She typically dressed in shorts and tied her hair up in a ponytail, accentuating her petite frame. Whenever I saw her, my eyes would inevitably be drawn to her, despite not intending it. I particularly admired her serene and beautiful demeanour, which surpassed that of other women in the neighbourhood.

Maria, a freelance graphic designer, worked from home while I was employed at a finance company located a 20-minute walk away from home. As a result, the time she would walk her dog happened to coincide with my departure to the office. It was a regular occurrence to see her walking Drogo, her gray-coloured Doberman. I often had concerns about Drogo accidentally getting off his leash, but I managed to remain calm.

It's strange, but walking behind Maria on those occasions developed within me a fondness for Drogo as well. It was purely coincidental that our paths aligned during the time she walked her dog while I headed to the office. Outside of that, I didn't harbour any specific desire to walk alongside or behind Maria.

Today unfolded like any other day. Maria was walking ahead of me, while I trailed behind, lost in my own thoughts and carrying my laptop bag. Unexpectedly, Drogo took notice of my bag and approached me. I moved to the sidewalk, attempting to cross the road, but the swift flow of cars made it difficult for me to do so. Unaware of Drogo nudging me, I didn't respond until Maria softly called out, "Sorry, please go ahead." She paused briefly, smiled at me, and gestured for me to proceed as we exchanged smiles.

Part of me wanted to pause and engage in a meaningful conversation, but my conscience and rationality restrained me. With age, I had grown wiser than my younger self. Memories of my college days in Nepal resurfaced, when I used to approach girls confidently in my early twenties. However, those encounters weren't limited to mere conversations. Influenced by friends, I even engaged in inappropriate behaviour like eve-teasing. Reflecting on those memories now filled me with shame and sent shivers down my spine. I realised how embarrassing and disrespectful those actions were. Perhaps the absence of having sisters of my own played a role in my behaviour, alongside the bad influence of my friends' company.

After completing college, I immigrated to the UK, where harassing girls was absolutely unthinkable. Instead, I underwent a significant transformation in my behaviour towards women. Whether it was being respectful and courteous to female colleagues in the workplace, giving them priority when traveling, or offering assistance whenever needed, I found myself adopting a more civilised approach. Throughout, I encountered numerous uncomfortable situations, but they never shook me or my mindset.

Just last week, while traveling on a train, I noticed a young woman sitting there, casually applying makeup. She effortlessly went through the routine of foundation, concealer, powder, kohl, eyeliner, and lipstick, occasionally checking herself in a small handheld mirror. Perhaps she caught me observing her, as I couldn't help but stare without inhibition. I thought that she had a naturally beautiful face and probably didn't need makeup. It was a common sight on public buses and trains in London, but my gaze remained fixated on her. Suddenly, my focus was shattered by the woman's loud scream. She snapped at me, "Have you never seen a girl before? Or a girl applying makeup?" It seemed like she was furious with me. I promptly stood up and left the train without saying a word.

Once again, I encountered Maria on the street today, following the same routine. She walked ahead of me, leading Drogo by her side. As Drogo defecated on the sidewalk, Maria promptly pulled out a tissue from her pocket. She used it to pick up the waste and placed it back in her pocket. A short distance away, she disposed of the tissue in a container labelled as 'Dog Foul'.' These containers were a common sight in the UK, as responsible dog owners were expected to dispose of their pet's waste properly. This practice not only avoided the risk of a £50 penalty but also reflected a mix of human habits, social responsibility, and love for dogs. With these thoughts in mind, I continued my walk.

In the meantime, memories of my past actions resurfaced vividly. I recalled how, back in Nepal, I used to thoughtlessly discard mandarin skins and peanut shells in public transportation while commuting to college. Reflecting on this, I felt disappointed in myself for my lack of social responsibility. It was evident how weak I had been in upholding such basic courtesy. While Maria and I may have shared the same walking path, our behaviours were distinctly different. Over time, I was gradually learning and improving upon these aspects.

Every day, I found myself increasingly drawn to Maria. However, I was unsure if this attraction merely stemmed from a desire for friendship or if it represented genuine love for her. I was caught in a state of confusion regarding my own feelings. Following Sabita's death, I had found myself completely alone in this unfamiliar world.

It had been seven long years since Sabita passed away. While the pangs of loneliness would occasionally affect me, I had grown accustomed to this solitary existence. In her final moments, Sabita had asked me, "Find a woman who loves you and get married. Don't just live with my memories." If living were as simple as she made it sound, I wouldn't have yearned for death so often. However, even the act of dying wasn't as easy as it seemed.

During Sabita's battle with cancer, I had become emotionally detached from life. Instead of being the one to console her, she comforted and inspired me to keep living. We had shared countless dreams, but they all faded away. For the past seven years, I have been trapped in a monotonous routine, shuttling back and forth between the office and home. Yet, I hadn't forgotten Sabita, nor did I wish to. While I had had several romantic affairs in the past, I had married only Sabita, and I had no desire to experience that aspect of married life again.

However, in Maria, I found glimpses of Sabita appearing again and again. The same serene and unassuming demeanour, accompanied by that gentle smile. Was I searching for Sabita within Maria? This question continued to resurface in my mind.

Recently, the brief encounters and walks with Maria on the streets had become less frequent, leaving me feeling somewhat saddened. In her absence, my eyes instinctively searched for her. I wondered if Maria's eyes also sought me out when I wasn't around. I was eager to find out.

However, I had stopped seeing Maria at our usual time in the morning. Instead, a minivan labelled 'Dog Daycare' would arrive to pick up Drogo each morning. As for Maria herself, I had no knowledge of where she went or what she did during the day. I had never taken a particular interest in her personal affairs, except for the times when she walked Drogo ahead or behind me.

***

Days passed, and my restlessness grew. It felt as if the reflection of my beloved Sabita was once again slipping away from me. Then, one day, I fell ill and couldn't go to work. To my surprise, the doorbell rang, and a courier stood at my doorstep with a package addressed to House No. 12. My heart leaped with joy when the courier confirmed that the package belonged to Maria. The arrival of the package symbolised Maria's presence in its entirety. Anticipating Maria's arrival in the evening to collect the package, my excitement knew no bounds. I wouldn't miss this opportunity to inquire about her well-being and reconnect with her.

As the doorbell rang, I quickly made my way to the door. Despite my illness, I had taken the time to shave and tidy up my appearance, eagerly anticipating Maria's possible visit in the evening.

When the doorbell chimed, my heart skipped a beat. And there she stood, Maria, bringing an instant delight to my day.

"Did my parcel get sent here?" Maria inquired, her gentle smile lighting up the room. I retrieved the package that was placed on the table and handed it to her. The thought of inviting her in for a cup of tea crossed my mind, but I hesitated. This was not Nepal, where inviting someone into your home for a warm conversation over tea was commonplace. Besides, she was a woman. Contemplating the possible interpretations of such an invitation, I decided to keep it to myself.

As I handed her the parcel, Maria offered a smile and said, "Thank you!" Her words stirred a series of emotions within me. Seizing the moment, I eagerly inquired, "Don't you work from home these days? How is your work going?"

"I've actually started working full-time at a company," she replied, her smile gentle yet accompanied by a hint of something distant. Her blue eyes appeared colder today, perhaps reflecting the accumulation of my own cold experiences. But then again, I could be mistaken. With these thoughts swirling in my mind, I bid Maria farewell. As I glanced at Sabita's photograph hanging in the living room, a wave of misery washed over me. In the span of seven years, I hadn't found anyone who came close to filling the void left by Sabita. Yet, I sensed fragments of Sabita within Maria, though I couldn't be entirely certain.

While Maria was no longer seen walking down the street on weekdays, she consistently appeared during weekends at the same time. However, I hesitated to emerge from my house at that specific time when she walked by. It seemed natural during my office hours, but during the weekends, purposelessly following her felt out of place. Moreover, I couldn't deny that this stage of life wasn't suitable for me to be trailing a woman on the streets. I couldn't reveal my feelings to Maria either; perhaps I believed the right time would present itself eventually.

On a Friday evening, my phone kept ringing incessantly. As expected, it was Bibek calling.

"Nishan, aren't you coming over today?" Bibek asked.

"Why don't you come to my place this time?" I replied, exhaling deeply.

"No problem!" Bibek responded, thankfully willing to make the journey to my place. I felt a sense of relief hearing that. My mind was reluctant to go anywhere. Whenever I visited Bibek's place, I ended up staying the entire weekend. I hadn't seen Maria walking Drogo on days other than Saturday and Sunday, one of the reasons why I lacked enthusiasm for visiting Bibek and his family. In fact, I did not want to miss the chance of seeing Maria on the weekend.

Bibek was my closest friend, the only person I could truly call my own in this foreign country. Before she passed away, Sabita had entrusted him with the responsibility of taking care of me. To prevent me from succumbing to loneliness, Bibek would often invite me to his place, and every Friday after work, I would pay him a visit. Spending time with Bibek, enjoying the meals prepared by his wife Seema, engaging in conversations, and playing with their two young children made the weekends fly by without me even realising it.

That's how my days passed by. Without someone to talk to in this country, I would have gone insane. The few English conversations I had at work were not enough for someone like me. No matter how much I spoke in English, it never satisfied my craving for conversation. During the weekends at Bibek's house, I would unleash all my thoughts and desires, finding solace in expressing myself freely.

In Nepal, I used to take pride in speaking English. Whenever a foreigner visited our office, I felt a surge of confidence as I showcased my English skills. But now, the tables had turned. I felt sick when I couldn't speak Nepali. It was only after waiting for 4-5 days that I would find solace at Bibek's house, where I could finally converse in my mother tongue.

Bibek had suggested that I look for work in his neighbourhood. I did consider it, but ultimately it made more sense for me to live close to my workplace rather than search for a job near his house. After all, it was only a matter of five days that I stayed at home.

Over the past few years, Bibek had been facing challenges due to a medical condition that limited his mobility. As a result, he spent the majority of his time confined to his home. I found comfort in the fact that I could offer him companionship, just as he provided me with his company.

Sometimes, when I played football with his kids, I would catch Bibek staring at us. This made me feel sorry for him but at the same time happy that he was in the UK, where the government provided regular financial support for his well-being. If he were in Nepal, his life would have been much more miserable. These thoughts weighed heavily on my mind. I could see him watching us as we played football at his house. I knew deep down how much he longed to join in and play with his kids, but circumstances and fate were not in his favour. My heart remained silent, understanding the pain he must have felt.

Bibek came to stay with me for a couple of days, and I went to the train station to pick him up. He arrived comfortably seated in a wheelchair. During his stay, we had conversations that often revolved around Maria. Whenever I spoke about her, Bibek would encourage me to express my feelings to her. However, I was filled with fear. The thought of being rejected by Maria was daunting, and I found more satisfaction in the simple greetings we exchanged on the streets than facing potential rejection.

As I was getting ready to go for a morning walk alone, Bibek insisted on joining me. He expressed his desire to see Maria at least once while he was here, and I couldn't refuse his request. So, we set off together, with Bibek in his wheelchair and me walking alongside him.

It was 8 a.m. My eyes instantly lit up as I spotted Maria approaching from the opposite side of the street, with Drogo by her side. Our eyes met, and it seemed like Maria paused for a moment as well. In that instant, I knew it was time to unlock my feelings for her.

With that thought in mind, I continued walking ahead, while Bibek maintained his own pace in the wheelchair. Suddenly, Drogo managed to slip out of Maria's grip and started running towards us. Witnessing this scene, Bibek, typically gripped by a profound fear of dogs, hastily abandoned the wheelchair, swiftly crossing the street in a surge of heightened urgency. I watched in astonishment as Bibek, who I had only seen crawl a few steps before to reach the bathroom, walked away due to his fear of the dog. Meanwhile, Maria attempted to secure Drogo back on the leash. Bibek, now on the other side of the street, began making his way back towards us once again.

"Try to be responsible! Can't you leash the dog properly?" Bibek immediately launched a verbal attack on Maria. It seemed that he couldn't fully understand or appreciate the unexpected situation and the resulting consequences that led him to walk.

"I apologise, I didn't mean to hurt you," Maria responded sincerely.

"At least, think of the disabled!" Bibek screamed. Maria chose not to respond and quietly muttered indistinct words while she departed with Drogo. Although I didn't intend to eavesdrop, I managed to catch a few discernible words amidst her mumbling.

"Disabled?"

"Looks like a benefit fraud. Bloody immigrants!"

I was stunned, feeling a sensation akin to plummeting from the sky. The contemptuous tone in her voice towards immigrants like us left me astounded. It was in that moment that I truly understood the significance of her cold, blue eyes. The affection and attraction I had developed for Maria over the course of several months suddenly vanished with just one sentence. Karma had truly come back around for my past misdeeds.

Memories of my college friends Kamlesh Shah and Bimalesh Shah surfaced, whom I used to harass by labelling them with the derogatory term 'Madishe'. I realised that I hadn't even shown respect to our fellow

Madhesi brothers, who hailed from the same country as us. Demanding that same respect in a foreign land didn't seem justified. I contemplated packing my bags and returning to Nepal immediately, but life wasn't that simple.

Today, I was profoundly saddened by the news about Bibek in a local newspaper. It turned out that he had been under surveillance for quite some time. Bibek, who had grown accustomed to relying on government benefits instead of working, was exposed through the newspaper. As a consequence, he was obligated to repay the entire amount he had deceitfully received and was given a ten-month prison sentence.

I found myself lacking the courage to either call Bibek or confront Maria on the streets.

**

The Wheel of Time

Everyone has their own life to live, though its meaning differs from person to person. Nevertheless, life remains a constant. When I observe someone unfamiliar to me, their life appears happy. With someone I know to some extent, their life seems somewhat satisfying. However, when it comes to my own life, which I am fully familiar with, I am completely dissatisfied. As I dive into the reality and truth of life, and as sadness takes hold, meeting Sushila has only added fuel to this fire of sorrow.

I am a man, and though I still carry pride in my heritage, I have already been defeated. Perhaps it's a consequence of Sushila's tears, like a curse that keeps pushing me on the verge of downfall. I have come to accept that one's deeds—both good and bad—are experienced within this lifetime.

Today, after encountering Sushila on the road, my sadness has deepened. She rushed towards me and implored, "Narendra! I want to be loved. I am your wife." I was taken aback and ran away, unable to comprehend what had happened to her. I don't know if Sushila is truly my wife. I lack the emotions expected of a husband, so how can she be my wife? Furthermore, we have never lived together.

This is our third meeting, but it has been a decade since our last encounter. We did not exchange a single word and I deeply regret this. Sushila seems to have lost her sanity, wearing torn clothes and dishevelled hair. Despite her half-mad state, I am astonished that she managed to recognise me.

I am to blame for Sushila's descent into madness. It was my ego that refused to accept her as my wife, even after performing the rituals of applying sindoor (vermilion) and adorning her with a mangalsutra[18]. However, I had no shortage of potential marriage partners. Perhaps that is why marrying Sushila felt like a mere game to me.

No matter how many times a man marries, the laws and societal rules in Nepal cannot govern his actions. Polygamy is deemed a crime, yet I unknowingly fell into its trap without much interest. My union with Sushila was solely motivated by the desire to acquire a large plot of land.

I carried a different pain in not being able to accept her as my wife, but Rashmi, the woman I loved and had high expectations from, betrayed me in unimaginable ways. It was only after Rashmi disappeared, taking away all my wealth, that I finally realised the truth. My dream of becoming a millionaire through marriage to Sushila was shattered, and I lost everything, descending into destitution.

---

[18] *The mangalsutra is a sacred necklace worn by married Hindu women, symbolising marital unity and the auspicious bond between husband and wife.*

I am ashamed of myself! What kind of person am I? Despite being consumed by remorse, I ran away from Sushila out of fear of losing respect. Now, besides my empty vanity, what else remains? I have put my very existence and self-esteem up for auction. My principle of "as long as you have fingers, you will have rings" is now buried somewhere in the past. I had experienced enough from my two previous marriages, and Sushila's marriage terrified me. I could never gather the courage to approach her, especially after seeing her partially burnt face.

Sushila appeared fine in the photographs. Even when I saw her from a distance, she still seemed fine. I didn't want to question or challenge anything after her family enticed me with the promise of land ownership, but the reality couldn't remain hidden from me. During one of the wedding rituals, I caught a glimpse of her face hidden beneath a veil, and my heartbeat paused briefly. The wedding proceeded, and when the veil was lifted, I felt as if I had fallen from the sky.

Sushila sent me numerous letters and messages. Her mother pleaded at my feet, begging for her daughter's honour. I was not someone who would easily be manipulated to become a scapegoat for others. That's why I remained unmoved.

In truth, I never intended to betray Sushila knowingly. Despite my belief that a woman's beauty is not everything, I was compelled to act. Thus, I escaped from life, from struggles, and from my compassion. Today, my empathy towards Sushila has multiplied. Sushila had lost part of her sanity, and if my days continue like this, I too will become insane. Not just partially, but completely insane.

Sushila's condition torments me, and Rashmi's betrayal haunts me. In the end, I gained nothing. No wealth, no love, and no sympathy from anyone. I am trapped within myself. I am crushed under the weight of sorrow. I don't know if I will ever cross paths with Sushila again in the twists and turns of life. I betrayed Sushila, and Rashmi betrayed me. Sometimes I cry, and sometimes I laugh, believing that I deserve all of this.

I realise that my mind has already embarked on the road to insanity. I foresee a tragic end awaiting me. It is inevitable that I will be consumed by this wheel of time.

***

Ram Maya

Everyone called her Sahuni[19]. I didn't know her real name either, but for a few years now, I had seen her bustling about in a small tea shop on a corner of New Road, at the heart of Kathmandu. At home, when my parents said, "There's not a single decent girl in this neighbourhood," I would casually reply, "Well, we have that tea shop girl."

Ever since the tea shop came into existence, everyone in the locality knew her. With her arrival, even the wayward lads who idled aimlessly on the streets would forsake their flirtations with passing girls and flock around her shop. No wonder her shop sold more than two hundred cups of tea a day.

Indeed! That poor tea shop girl, who had not received any special favour from destiny, had an exceptional charm even in her worn-out clothes and plain appearance. She looked barely seventeen or eighteen but possessed a youthful charm that surpassed her age. She stood amidst a cabinet with five glasses, a teapot, a stove, and a small bench in the middle, diligently brewing tea.

As I passed by her shop, I couldn't help but steal glances at her. Her presence stirred waves of emotions even in my

[19] *A female shopkeeper*

feminine heart. Like flies buzzing around, the lads would sit huddled on the bench sipping tea. But the abusive remarks cast upon her a couple of days back struck me deeply.

"What a whore she is, corrupting my son! She needs to be kicked out of this neighbourhood." These heartless words of Shil Bahadur evoked sympathy in me towards woman everywhere. His morally corrupt son had attempted to rape a local girl Revati, for which he had spent about fifteen days behind bars. Sons of wealthy men like Shil Bahadur were known to exploit the dignity of poor girls, as they sought to buy and sell them for their own gains. And what is Sahuni's fault here? The teashop was her lifeline, yet people had so much to say about her.

And amidst the fuss, there still was a glimmer of hope that Shil Bahadur's son, though initially tainted by drug abuse, would seek redemption. However, some people never change, and the same predatory glint stayed with him. Seeing the tea shop closed for two weeks, I became increasingly anxious. On the streets, people started whispering, "Have you heard? Shil Bahadur said that she eloped with a guy named Ram Bahadur."

Days passed, and suddenly, four years later, I saw her on the cover of a magazine and was completely taken aback. As I took the magazine in my hand, the words "Ram Maya got AIDS" scared the life out of me. Sahuni's alias Ram Maya, had been sold in Mumbai and then forced into prostitution, and after being infected with AIDS, she was mercilessly thrown out. My heart ached at the thought of her youth consumed by the fiery blaze of the disease. What had been lacking in the life of someone as wealthy as Shil Bahadur that he resorted to such despicable crimes?

I took a deep breath and blinked my eyes in disbelief at the explosive headline. Oh! After Shil Bahadur's son made Ram Maya a victim of rape, to protect him from the clutches of the law, Shil Bahadur had tied her with the thread of false assurance of getting her married to his son, leaving her helpless in foreign soil. My heart sank deep.

And nowadays, whenever I happen to pass by the corner where Ram Maya's tea shop once stood, the echoes of her laughter resonate, and the memory of her first radiant smile lingers in my mind, intertwining with the blurry pages of the magazine.

***

The Compromise Within the Confrontation

"Good day, this is Director J.K. Bista speaking," greeted Jeevan Kumar Bista, known as J.K. Bista, constantly bombarded by phone calls. Rashmi settled comfortably in the lounge after moving from the kitchen. By the time she settled, Jeevan had already ended the call.

"Who was it?" Rashmi asked, placing a cup of steaming tea before Jeevan.

"I'm not sure, the call got disconnected," Jeevan replied, his eyes still fixed on the phone.

Jeevan took a sip of the tea, relishing its comforting warmth. He glanced out the window for a moment, as if someone were waiting outside. Despite the scorching heat in the quiet streets of the Greenacre neighbourhood in Croydon, not a single leaf stirred without a breeze. Regardless of the temperature, Jeevan's love for tea remained unwavering. It brought him joy that transcended seasons, whether in the embrace of summer or the chill of winter, he found solace in his daily ritual of enjoying twelve to fifteen cups of tea.

"I didn't hear the phone ring!" Rashmi interjected, a hint of surprise in her voice as she stood before Jeevan.

Jeevan remained silent, his gaze meeting Rashmi's in a moment of shared understanding. Though he refrained from speaking, his eyes conveyed volumes.

Perhaps Jeevan had a point, Rashmi thought silently. Just last week, she had visited the hospital to have her ears examined. Even now, her hearing was not at its best. Was it the toll of time or an underlying issue? The results of her ear examination had not arrived yet, leaving her with unanswered questions.

Rashmi reminisced about her younger days when her sharp ears caught even the faintest whispers, making her friends and family cautious about being overheard. She remembered how she could hear the conversations in the kitchen from her bedroom and grasp what her friends were whispering in a corner of the classroom. They would sometimes playfully encourage Rashmi to eavesdrop on school gossip. Rashmi couldn't help but smile at those mischievous memories from childhood.

On a Monday morning, Rashmi took a day off from work to take her sick daughter to the doctor. It was challenging to quickly find someone to help in a foreign land. Moreover, Jeevan was always engrossed in his work. Rashmi felt that she had less understanding of what was happening in Jeevan's life.

Jeevan had a strong sense of responsibility towards their children, but life hadn't been very kind to him abroad. Many times, he felt like returning to Nepal and leaving everything and everyone behind. However, even in Nepal, he had no one. Both his parents had passed away in an earthquake, and their house was destroyed in the tragedy. Besides the broken remnants of the house and the desolate land, he had nothing of his own in Nepal. Relatives were there, but they seemed to have vanished in the vortex of life.

Rashmi had grown up in an orphanage, so she had no family ties. All she considered her own were Jeevan and their two children. She had received education support from her foreign foster father, Chris, who helped her study in a boarding school in Kathmandu and pursue higher education at a university. She excelled in her studies and had a good command of English. With an officer-level job in Nepal, she had never thought of permanently settling abroad. However, after marriage and at Jeevan's insistence, she had come to the UK. She quickly secured a job in a non-governmental organisation, a position she considered below her qualifications, but she needed a job to start a life. Even though the salary wasn't high, Rashmi's income supported the family. As for Jeevan, he was constantly searching for work; however, he refused to settle for low-level jobs.

"Good morning, this is Director J.K. Bista speaking," Jeevan immersed himself in another phone conversation, while Rashmi struggled to hear amidst the blaring TV volume.

It was already ten in the morning, time to take their daughter to the doctor. Rashmi hesitated to leave the son alone, finding comfort when the children were together. Last week, a neighbour had found their daughter Kalpana wandering towards the street and handed her over to

Jeevan. Rashmi only discovered this incident when the neighbour sternly warned her to be more careful in the future.

"If this happens again, I will report it to the police. It seems you can't properly look after your kids," the neighbour's threatening remarks left Rashmi stressed.

Their son Kamal sat on the sofa, engrossed in the TV, while the daughter cried incessantly. Rashmi didn't even have time to get ready herself, let alone prepare the daughter. Who could she ask for help? No one. Unlike Nepal, they didn't have domestic workers in their homes, nor were there any other family members around. Jeevan was her sole companion.

"Jeevan, why don't you take a break from work? And please, pay some attention to the children," Rashmi suggested gently, her gaze fixed on Jeevan. Although Rashmi spoke softly, even those words became hard for Jeevan to bear.

"Are you teaching me how to take care of the children now? Who raised our four-year-old son and three-year-old daughter? Wasn't it this houseboy, Jeevan Kumar Bista? Outside, I may be J.K. Bista, the Director, but inside our home, I am your servant, Jeevan Kumar Bista. You have done a great favour by shouldering the financial burden of your husband, household, and family, haven't you?" Jeevan sarcastically snapped, his words expressing years of bottled-up emotions.

"I didn't mean it like that! I understand that you devote a significant amount of time to the children. I was simply expressing my concern that sometimes, when you become engrossed in your work, you may unintentionally neglect everything else," Rashmi explained apologetically, feeling remorseful for her words.

"You're right. I don't have a job like yours. I can't earn money as you do. You're the one providing meals for us. You must feel proud of that, right?" Jeevan threw the newspaper to the ground and walked into the kitchen.

"Now I understand! Your frustration is aimed at me just because I didn't do the dishes, right?" Jeevan clanged pots and pans in the kitchen sink, starting to clean them.

Lost in her thoughts, Rashmi remained silent in the living room. Once upon a time, life was blissful and content for Jeevan and Rashmi. Jeevan came from an upper-middle-class family, with everything at his disposal before they moved to the UK. He never had to compromise—good education, a prestigious director position in an international non-governmental organisation, a comfortable income, and a happy family were all part of Jeevan's life. However, the allure of foreign lands and the desire for greater financial success drove him to leave it all behind.

The reality struck hard when Jeevan set foot in the UK, and he never anticipated having to adapt to this new reality. Three long years were spent searching for employment, tirelessly sending out countless applications, hoping for a breakthrough. While he managed to secure interviews for some of these opportunities, they ultimately proved fruitless. These three years were no less demanding than a full-time job for Jeevan, revolving around browsing websites, tailoring resumes, sending applications, and occasionally attending interviews. In this relentless quest for a job that aligned with his education and experience, Jeevan frequently found himself overcome by exhaustion, and he would unknowingly doze off to sleep, only to wake up and repeat the cycle the next morning. Unaware of what the future held in store for him, Jeevan remained oblivious to the unfolding chapters of his life.

Jeevan had friends who, like him, had sound academic degrees but were working at places like McDonald's, restaurants, and security jobs. One of his dear friends, Kiran, even became a taxi driver, but Jeevan's self-esteem prevented him from embracing such roles. Instead, two years ago, he bravely started J.K. Consultancy. It earned him respect within society and bestowed a sense of dignity. With the title on his business card, Jeevan could hold his head high in front of acquaintances, friends, and fellow Nepali individuals.

Though he once considered doing small jobs to ease Rashmi's financial burden, the fear of being recognised by acquaintances and fellow Nepalese at work deterred him. Instead, he remained determined to propel J.K. Consultancy forward, working tirelessly in the hopes of success. The saga of his financial failure remained confined to the walls of their home, whereas to the outer world, it seemed like a happy family of four. There was no need to justify who earned more between husband and wife. However, the weight of economic responsibility that

Rashmi had to bear tormented Jeevan's soul. Uncertain about what lay ahead, he couldn't help but shed tears of frustration and self-doubt, feeling defeated by his perceived failures. Seeking help, he even attended counselling sessions and took medication to fight off the depression that consumed him. Yet, he never lost faith that J.K. Consultancy would one day flourish.

Although time passed swiftly, Jeevan's unwavering spirit and dedication to climb the ladder of success remained intact. His efforts knew no bounds. Recently, however, Rashmi had been feeling slightly uneasy. Despite the reassurance from her ear examination report that her hearing was fine, she couldn't shake off the feeling that something ominous was about to happen whenever the phone rang or was answered.

"Hello! Director J.K. Bista speaking." These words once again captured Rashmi's attention. Lately, she found herself listening more intently to these words.

"Whose call is it, Jeevan?" Rashmi asked curiously.

These days, when Jeevan answered the phone, Rashmi's heart would skip a beat, and she would tremble with fear. Nervousness fluttered in her eyes as she wondered if her hearing had weakened, but even that notion proved false.

"It's just a marketing promotion. Maybe our phone number and consultancy name are listed in the local directory, leading to more calls," Jeevan replied, smiling.

In that smile, it seemed as if Jeevan had discovered a flicker of hope for a brighter future. His optimism appeared to have grown stronger. In this moment, his smile at least appeared sincere. However, Jeevan remained unaware of his own inner turmoil, envisioning the success of his consultancy despite his troubled mental state. Answering calls, taking notes, and preparing reports kept him busy continuously. It appeared that Jeevan was exceptionally occupied, even answering phone calls more frequently.

"Hello! Director J.K. Bista speaking," Jeevan answered the phone again, his smile widening.

"Jeevan, the phone isn't ringing. I haven't been to the office for two weeks. It's been 14 days since this landline last rang," tears welled up in Rashmi's eyes once again.

Jeevan couldn't compromise his self-esteem, but in doing so, he had succumbed to mental illness. Meanwhile, Rashmi had to take a break from work to care for their young children and her emotionally fragile husband. She felt lost and uncertain about how to move forward in life. Concrete plans eluded her, and her tears continued to flow unabated.

***

Extraordinary Death

The relentless ringing of a bicycle bell outside momentarily disrupted my composure but my agitation subsided when I realised it was the postman at the door. There is nothing that brings me greater joy than receiving a letter. How can one not treasure the opportunity to share heartfelt affection with distant loved ones? As someone living in a foreign land, there are times when I yearn to return home after completing my studies, to immerse myself in the love of my dear ones. However, I cannot disregard my future for moments of fleeting affection. Thus, I walk patiently alongside the time, now entering the fourth year of my medical studies in India.

But today holds a significance beyond compare. When the postman delivered Binita's letter this morning, it elevated me to cloud nine. Even as I unfold the pages of Binita's letter, my hands tremble with anticipation. I always hope that her words bear no traces of her hardships. Those blissful days spent with her, the moments woven within our friendship, and her wedding... they all stir a sense of unease. Everything gradually unfolds before my eyes. My love was never intended to limit her within the confines of my memories for my own selfish desires. During those fleeting moments, I adorned her within the realms of my dreams. Yet, after her marriage, I find solace in envisioning her happiness, her laughter, and more. When she shares that her husband loves her deeply, it brings me immense joy, while also prompting me to ask myself, "More than I ever could?" Love exists within the boundaries of marriage, a truth not unfamiliar. Love also exists between two lovers, another undeniable reality. Yet, this unrequited love, this one-sided sacrifice, where I am lost within the chambers of her memory and imagination, that is love in its truest form.

Anyway, Binita's letter has arrived from Kathmandu, a testament to our genuine friendship. Binita is different from others, setting her apart. That is why our bond remains unyielding. Oh, as I delve into the pages of the past, I inadvertently overlook the present. And when I reside in the present, the past slips from my mind. How strange are these habits of mine! Setting aside all imaginings, I focus on reading the letter. However, her greeting catches me off guard. In her previous letters, she simply wrote "Dear Nishan," but this time, she has added the prefix "My," leaving me weightless, as if floating in the sky. Yes, I am melting within her presence. Emotions surge and intertwine within my mind, causing my hands to tremble. The words etched in Binita's letter bring me profound elation.

My dear Nishan,

I must share some news with you that might come as a surprise. I am separating from my husband. He wants this, and you know why? Because he thinks I am no longer able to fulfil his physical, mental, and financial needs. Currently, I am supporting myself with money from my parents, and since the required treatment is not available here, I am coming to Bangalore[20]. Perhaps I will meet you there. However, I might not survive more than six months. Whether these words should be written in a letter or not, I am unsure, but as a true friend and a medical student, I feel it is necessary to inform you that I have been diagnosed with "blood cancer." I am not afraid of my own death. I wish for it to come swiftly so that its impact on your life can be minimised.

I am a married woman, and I had hoped to die with that honour, but my husband's divorce advice has already shattered me. It feels like a murder every time I am labelled as the "Cancer girl" in the neighbourhood. I hope you understand me. I have a purpose behind sharing this lengthy letter and bringing you face-to-face with reality. Please, Nishan! Make cancer your field of study. At least for my sake, become that great doctor and save other cancer patients. After marriage, please love your wife, but don't confine that love to your selfish needs. Women have souls too, and they ache with cutting words, just like mine. By the time I receive a reply to this letter, I might already be divorced. I often wonder if "cancer" is the consequence of past-life sins. If not, why am I destined to suffer like this? If God exists and reincarnation is real, I pray to be reborn as a woman because enduring abuse seems preferable over being afflicted by this ailment.

I apologise if my words have caused you discomfort because you are a man. But I assure you, I don't mean to

[20]   *Bangalore, currently known as Bengaluru, is a bustling metropolis in southern India.*

offend you. These words stem from my current condition and the waves of inner turmoil. I understand that not all men are the same, and I hold you in high regard among them. If only I possessed the sacrifice, dedication, self-awareness, and understanding that you have, I wouldn't have succumbed to this abnormal death. Everyone must face death one day, but people deserve more peace in dying than in living, a state I am far from experiencing. My heart is heavy, and my mind is loaded down. I am uncertain whether I can bear the weight of tomorrow's divorce, as my husband is getting remarried the day after. Because of my cancer, I have become a burden to him, and he seeks a divorce to avoid legal complications. Where can I turn to beg for the love that the marriage is supposed to bring? I have nowhere to turn, only my self-respect remains. Unable to find a proper place to alleviate the growing pain in my heart, I reach out to you. Please forgive me for my choice of words.

That's all for today.

Yours sincerely,

Binita

The letter slips from my hand and unexpectedly falls to the ground. My heart sinks. I'm astonished by the cruelty Binita has endured from her husband. Although some of her words may have stung me, she spoke the truth. If I were in her position, I would likely have expressed the same sentiments. It is disheartening to see that many men exploit their rights. However, before causing harm to others, men should imagine themselves enduring such cruelty.

If Binita were my wife, words could not express how much I would have loved her. I would have fulfilled her every wish. I would have made Binita experience the extent to which men can embody sacrifice and devotion, teaching her that a husband doesn't possess his wife, but rather cherishes her as his heartbeat, as a soulmate. But what can I do? I am helpless. I can only pray for her to have a painless death.

Today, I recall the words Binita once shared during our time in college, "I don't want to die an ordinary death. I want to contribute something to the country and the nation before I die." Her unwavering determination has now shattered like a mirror. However, she has found an extraordinary death that surpasses even her own imagination. A death that combines the anguish of abuse, cancer, and a broken marriage.

***

The Mindset Nurtured by Solitude

The clothing store on the ground floor of a tall, gigantic building in the busy city of Sydney was bustling with activity. Sarjala was fully occupied, selling a variety of shoes and clothing items to the customers. Amidst the hustle and bustle, she momentarily lost track of her exhaustion.

A young woman entered the fitting room, trying on dresses and seeking Sarjala's opinion as she repeatedly went in and out. Sarjala couldn't help but smile at the woman's playful restlessness. Eventually, the woman found satisfaction with the last dress she tried on. Sarjala had been giving her special attention—standing out among the crowd in the shop. The reason behind this special treatment was the young woman's polite demeanour and engaging conversation.

During their introduction, Sarjala shared her name, and the woman, Jennifer, introduced herself with a gentle smile. Holding the dress in her hand, Jennifer said, "Guess what, Sarjala? If my boyfriend doesn't like this dress, I'll be very disappointed!"

Sarjala, providing a more personal touch beyond her role as a shopkeeper, replied, "You look amazing in it!" Jennifer was overjoyed upon hearing Sarjala's words.

"Can I return this dress if my boyfriend doesn't like it?" Jennifer asked eagerly.

"Of course, you can. Just make sure you don't take long," Sarjala replied, offering a kind smile.

"Thank you! By the way, do you have a boyfriend?" Jennifer asked hesitantly.

"Nope!" Sarjala honestly revealed.

Throughout her life, the feeling of falling in love had been foreign to her. The concept of love didn't even register in her mind, as she tended to embrace a more pessimistic outlook. Witnessing the successive breakups of her friends' relationships had left her disheartened. At the age of fourteen, she moved to Sydney with her parents, attending school and working at her father's shop. Now, at the age of nineteen, she remained distanced from the realm of romantic entanglements.

Her fourteen years in Nepal had instilled within her a cultural perspective that emphasised the idea that true love transcended superficial appearances. While her friends enjoyed outings with their boyfriends, she too yearned for a similar experience. She imagined having a boyfriend in her life, but things never seemed to work out. It wasn't that boys didn't show interest in her, but before committing to a relationship, she sought assurance of their genuine love. Unfortunately, the boys would disappoint her by attempting to be physically forward or intimate before she could even decide. In spite of her wish, she hadn't been able to adopt a Western mindset. Her foreign friends viewed her solitary life as naive and meaningless, but she couldn't change who she was.

Jennifer's recent inquiry struck a familiar chord and hurt her just as before. After much deliberation, she truthfully responded, "No, I don't have a boyfriend. It simply hasn't happened for me."

"You really caught me off guard with that!" Jennifer expressed her astonishment at Sarjala's revelation. In her culture, it was acceptable to not have a boyfriend for a certain period, but even as she approached the end of her vibrant teenage years, the idea of not having a boyfriend seemed like a joke.

"Well, make sure you have a boyfriend the next time I visit here! Wish you all the best," Jennifer playfully winked her eye. Carrying the bag containing her dress, she bid farewell and left.

Jennifer did not return the following day, and Sarjala assumed that Jennifer's boyfriend must have liked the dress, bringing her great joy. Perhaps Jennifer had simply forgotten about Sarjala, but Sarjala couldn't forget her. Jennifer's parting words lingered in her mind, haunting her during the solitary hours of the night, serving as a constant reminder.

Sarjala's parents were unaware of this situation. They were not parents brought up in Western cultures who, tired of their daughter's single status, would assist her in finding a boyfriend. Moreover, their values and principles prevented them from doing so. Sarjala had not yet reached the age of marriage, and she herself had no interest in getting married.

***

Amongst the throng of tourists gathered around the Opera House, Samar and Sarjala found themselves lost in their own world. Sarjala had finally found a Nepali boy, fulfilling her long-held desire. They stood together, gazing at the reflection of their vibrant dreams in the shimmering waters. The sea, in its expansive embrace, seemed to bestow its blessings upon their newfound love.

In the midst of the bustling crowd, Sarjala spotted Jennifer, the familiar face she had met three months ago, wearing the same dress she had purchased from Sarjala's store. However, Jennifer found it difficult to recognise Sarjala at first. Swiftly, Sarjala approached her and said, "Hi Jennifer! Do you remember me?"

"I have this strange feeling that we've met before, but I can't quite recall where..." Jennifer appeared confused.

"Can you remember where you bought this dress from?" Sarjala gestured towards the dress Jennifer was wearing.

"Oh my goodness! My memory fails me!" Jennifer chuckled.

"Guess what? I actually have a boyfriend now, but you never showed up at the store again... Meet my boyfriend, Samar," Sarjala said, pointing towards Samar.

"Congratulations!" Jennifer exclaimed with genuine excitement.

"And this is my boyfriend, Stuart!" Jennifer introduced her own companion.

"It seems we have similar tastes. Doesn't this dress look great on her, Stuart?" Sarjala asked, directing her gaze towards Stuart. Stuart hesitated briefly before responding.

"He's not my ex-boyfriend. We've only been dating for a week," Jennifer clarified.

"What happened to your ex?" Sarjala inquired.

"The relationship ended just two weeks after I visited your store," Jennifer replied with a light-hearted laugh, indicating that she wasn't bothered by it.

"And what about this dress?" Sarjala asked, expressing surprise and a hint of seriousness.

"It looks good, and it holds sentimental value for me," Jennifer replied with a gentle smile. Sarjala couldn't help but continue watching Jennifer until she disappeared from her sight.

It was around 10-11 o'clock in the morning, and Sarjala's store was calm and quiet. In that peaceful atmosphere, Sarjala was deeply lost in her own thoughts. She had been on a quest to find love, and finally, she succeeded. Frustrated with the constant interrogations and the need to prove her mental and physical well-being to others, she decided to commit herself to a relationship.

Like her friends, she now enjoyed going out with her boyfriend. Whether it was Samar accompanying her to the bus stop or meeting her at school, she felt a sense of pride and excitement in front of her friends. However, despite all this, she hadn't yet found the true love she had longed for.

***

Jennifer's arrival in the morning filled Sarjala with immense joy. Sarjala's happiness soared as she anticipated the opportunity to engage in meaningful conversations with Jennifer, free from the distractions of a crowded store.

"Can you please show me a nice pair of jeans and an off-white T-shirt? It's Stuart's favourite colour," Jennifer requested.

In response to Jennifer's request, Sarjala promptly presented her with a range of options. It didn't take long for Jennifer to find exactly what she was looking for.

"I must say, your shop is truly impressive! I always find exactly what I need," Jennifer exclaimed, expressing her sincere gratitude.

"Black seems to be your boyfriend's favourite colour, doesn't it? I always see you wearing black," Jennifer inquired, observing Sarjala.

"No, actually, it's my personal preference. I don't have a boyfriend anymore," Sarjala responded, feeling a tinge of disappointment.

"Has it ended already?" Jennifer asked, filled with curiosity.

"Yes," Sarjala forced a smile, concealing her inner pain, much like her friends did.

Despite living in a different country, she very much held onto her Nepali mindset. She had spent years searching for a suitable Nepali boyfriend. Unfortunately, Samar turned out to be a deceitful person, who had come abroad for work while leaving his wife behind in Nepal. His true intentions, driven by his physical desires in the absence of his wife, were exposed later on. Sarjala ended the relationship once she discovered his true nature.

Sarjala had undergone a noticeable transformation from her past self. Previously, her friends had doubted her mental and physical well-being, but she had proven them wrong by entering into a relationship like them. As a result, her friends had stopped pestering her. Although this provided some relief, Sarjala carried deep emotional wounds from past hurt and betrayal. Unlike her friends, she couldn't easily move on and jump into new relationships, nor could she abandon the comfort of wearing black clothes that provided solace during her times of pain.

***

Boundary of Ideals

Minu felt extremely anxious as she stood at the bus stop in Ratnapark, a crucial transportation hub in Kathmandu. She went restless like a fish wriggling out of water. She was willing to take any mode of transportation that came her way—whether it be a tempo, taxi, public bus, or minibus. However, she adhered strictly to a personal rule against accepting rides in private cars, a principle she held dear.

Despite her unwavering efforts and hard work, Minu found herself deeply frustrated by the constant setbacks she faced. As she waited, she wiped away her sweat with a handkerchief; not because it was too hot, but because the turmoil inside her was causing more distress than the heat. The process of waiting for a vehicle had only heightened her nervousness.

The sun shone brightly, and the 15–20-minute wait felt like an eternity. "Why did I have to miss the school bus today?" Minu sighed heavily. She had already attempted to board four buses, but the sight of people crammed inside made her feel even more frustrated. Time slipped away rapidly, and as a woman, she knew it wouldn't be easy for her to travel by hanging from the door of a crowded bus.

However, missing school was not an option for her today. On any other day, she would have likely returned home by now.

Private cars zoomed past, seemingly mocking her helplessness. Despite plenty of vehicles plying on the road, she was astonished at her inability to find space in any of them. Just then, a minibus came to a halt. Although it was already packed with passengers, noticing nobody hanging from the door, she reckoned she could manage to fit inside. Making her way through the back entrance, she squeezed herself into the crowded bus.

The bus conductor forcefully pushed her in, climbed aboard, slammed the door shut, and blew a loud whistle. No sooner, Minu found herself surrounded by a crowd of men, and fear gripped her suddenly.

The bus started moving, making stops at each bus station approximately every two minutes. However, the clock's hands moved at their own pace, indifferent to the bus's halts. Minu, a primary school teacher in her mid-twenties, had a sick husband at home, and lacking the skill to ride a scooter, she faced a challenge. Today marked the day when the school released the exam results and distributed report cards, intensifying her anxiety. The weight of her responsibilities bore down on her heavily. Nonetheless, she was determined to reach the school, even if it meant arriving late. This journey seemed arduous and challenging to her. Suddenly, she recalled the numerous obligations faced by countless women who had to travel daily in crowded public buses, standing among a sea of men.

Minu experienced extreme discomfort inside the bus. She made a concerted effort to distance herself from the persistent advances of grown men trying to get too close. She physically pushed some of them away and gave stern glares to the others as a warning. In the meantime, she had already passed three or four bus stops. Unlike her usual experience on the school bus, where children willingly offered their seats, today, no one seemed willing to give up their seat for her.

The struggle, however, wasn't exclusive to Minu; there was another woman with a child who was being squeezed by the crowded space. The child started wailing, contributing to the already suffocating atmosphere, which rapidly descended into chaos. Nearby passengers, now irritated, raised their voices, "Why bring a child like this on the bus?" The woman was preoccupied with trying to comfort her child, while Minu felt a surge of anger.

Frustrated, Minu suddenly lost her composure and yelled, "If not the bus, how else should we commute?" The boy sitting next to her glanced at Minu's face.

Abruptly, the bus came to a halt as the brakes were applied, causing the woman with the child to nearly stumble from the jolt. Minu quickly reached out to steady the child. Unable to endure the situation any longer, she turned to the man sitting in front of her and implored, "Brother, please give up your seat... Show some compassion for this woman with a small child."

"On the bus, countless women desperately need someone's kindness every day. Why don't you, sister, take it upon yourself to reserve a bus for them?" the boy heartlessly retorted, triggering laughter from everyone around. Minu felt deeply embarrassed. By that time, the crowd had pushed her towards the front of the bus.

"Sit properly... or else... do you see my nails? I'll scratch your face with them," a girl's voice from the crowd caught Minu's attention. It seemed as if the voice yearned for empathy. In that moment, Minu approached the girl and asked, "What's wrong, sister?"

"What else? I'm seething because of these rascals! I wonder if they have sisters at home! These men are like hungry wolves," the young girl exclaimed, filled with resentment.

"You're absolutely right, that's exactly how it is! Even if they're reported to the police, they rarely face proper consequences. No wonder they continue their behaviour with such impunity!" Minu began speaking passionately.

The young girl remained silent, seemingly deep in thought as she analysed Minu's words. Perhaps Minu's role as a teacher had accustomed her to speaking out. Minu continued, "Last year, I took some harassers to the police station for eve-teasing. They came from influential and wealthy families, and no wonder, they didn't face any punishment. Since then, I've lost trust in everyone except myself."

"You're absolutely right, sister. These men view women as objects for their pleasure, subjecting them to appalling acts like eve-teasing. The boys are never seen as immoral, but the girls who fight back are instantly labelled as having loose character. Isn't that the reality, sister?" The young woman joined Minu, their voices harmonising.

"Yes, that's how it is… we are expected to suffer in silence. What else can we do? What impact can our two voices make? Even the women empowerment centres in our society remain silent. They witness the issues faced by many women but choose not to recognise them as problems. No one speaks up. Who dares to raise their voice in this male-dominated society?" Minu seized the opportunity to express all her pent-up frustrations.

The unknown girl, now backed by Minu's support, appeared visibly amazed. Exuding quite a dignified persona, she alighted at her stop. As she stepped off the bus, the entire crowd inside the bus turned to look at her.

"What's the point of this senseless banter in such a suffocating atmosphere!" a man interjected abruptly.

In the absence of the young girl, Minu sensed a strong opposition. In that moment, she found herself engulfed in the sea of unfamiliar faces. Her previous resolute opinion began to wane and felt stifled without any backing. Enduring the pain of being a woman, she turned her attention to the woman with the child, who had already been pushed aside by the crowd, forced into an invisible corner. Her presence only resonated through the distant cries of her child.

Minu shot a disdainful look at the men on the bus. She felt the intrusion of personal space as one man behind her seemed to encroach, but with her stop approaching soon, she refrained from reacting strongly. She chose to endure his misbehaviour for a little while, making a promise to herself that she would leave home early from now on and never miss her school bus. Today's journey had already taken a toll on her, leaving her not just physically but also emotionally burdened by the mental torment inflicted by male passengers. Her female body, surrounded by men, teetered on the brink of crying out and exploding with frustration.

Minu took a deep breath, but she couldn't escape the sensation of a male hand inching closer to her. Despite her efforts to maintain distance, she was unable to ward off unwarranted touches throughout the bus journey. This unsettling pattern repeated itself, with her constantly being pushed from one side and retreating back to her previous position.

Fear raced through Minu's heart as a hand stealthily crept towards her from behind. Nervousness overcame her when the thick hand, seeking support from the metal handle near the window, came to rest on her shoulder. This time, Minu's anger knew no bounds. She channelled her frustration, unleashing it with her long, sharp nails to inflict a deep scratch on the intruding hand. A painful scream followed as the hand hastily withdrew from Minu's shoulder.

Intrigued by a somewhat familiar sound accompanying the scream, Minu turned to look back, curious to identify the person responsible. Peering through the crowded bus, Minu locked eyes with the man's face. To her disbelief, she recognised her brother-in-law standing there. A profound sense of fear consumed her, as if she were trapped in a terrifying nightmare. Her eyes involuntarily welled up, a mix of anger and disgust washing over her.

Minu was rendered speechless upon discovering her brother-in-law among the same category of predatory men. She couldn't bring herself to spit at him, nor could she muster tears. The contempt she felt was unprecedented, especially considering she had never regarded her relatives with such disdain. While her sister had hailed her husband as an ideal man, Minu was stunned to witness him crossing the boundaries of decency. The minibus fell into an abrupt silence at this moment, yet Minu's body burned with rage and indignation.

"It's you, brother-in-law? I never expected this from you," Minu's voice slipped unintentionally from her lips.

Caught off guard by the embarrassing and awkward situation, her brother-in-law was left dumbfounded, his hand gently caressing the scratches. Finally, he spoke, "Well, Minu, I didn't realise it was you."

"What if it was another woman in my position? Would that have been acceptable to you?" Minu fired back in anger.

Countless eyes in the crowd fixated on Minu and her brother-in-law, as if witnessing an intriguing drama unfold before them. Though her own eyes struggled to accept the reality, the collective gaze of the onlookers spoke volumes. A volcano of emotions simmered within her mind, on the brink of eruption. She could no longer bear the weight of the journey. Determined, she made up her mind to alight the bus before reaching her intended destination and hastily walked away.

***

Lauren's Daddies

"Kabita, hey Kabita! Why do you spend so much time staring out the window? If it's Saturday, you just hang around the window!" Usha found herself surprised by her seven-year-old daughter's habit of sitting glued to the window and gazing outside on Saturdays. She couldn't fathom what was going through Kabita's young mind, and while it didn't appear to be a serious concern, Usha was intrigued to understand why her daughter, known for her playful nature and dubbed 'Puckish Kabita' by her friends, had suddenly become quietly fixated on the window. This behaviour started only after they moved to the Greenacre neighbourhood about three months ago.

"Nothing, Mum! Just checking if Lauren is outside," Kabita replied, referring to the girl living next door.

"Then why do you keep staring outside? If you want to play, go ring her doorbell and invite her to play," Usha suggested.

Kabita didn't respond; she smiled gently and quickly grabbed her iPad and started watching cartoons.

Her mother Usha couldn't understand whether Kabita wanted to play outside or not. Every day after school, Kabita would usually join her friends from the neighbourhood and engage in hours of play, jumping and running, as if the word 'tiredness' didn't exist in her vocabulary. Usha was amazed by her daughter's boundless energy. Kabita preferred playing outdoors more than indoors. It was Usha's encouragement that had fostered Kabita's love for playing outside. Previously, Kabita would only occupy herself with devices like iPads, laptops, and mobile phones since she had no friends to play with.

When Usha and Prakash, Kabita's father, moved from their previous residence in Park Hill to the Greenacre neighbourhood near Kabita's school, they found themselves in Croydon town, where many families with young children lived. As a result, Kabita made new friends to play with. Throughout the week, Kabita appeared lively and active, except for Saturdays when she would retreat to the window and stare outside silently.

Usha was unsure of what Kabita was thinking. Days passed like this. Kabita's obsession with gazing out the window was limited to Saturdays initially, but over time, she started appearing serious on other days as well. Usha genuinely wanted to understand the reason behind Kabita's unusual behaviour and make her daughter happy again, but unfortunately, her efforts had been unsuccessful so far.

It was a hot day in July, even at five in the evening, the sun was shining brightly. Usha could hear the noise of children playing outside the house, but Kabita showed no excitement to go and join them.

"Kabita! Aren't you playing outside today?" Usha asked curiously.

"No, Mum. I'd rather draw some pictures," Kabita showed no enthusiasm or interest in going out to play.

"That's fine, dear. But tomorrow, after school, you're going out to play, understood?"

"Sure!" Kabita rushed to her room. She grabbed her sketchbook, pens, and coloured pencils.

The evening settled in. Usha hurriedly prepared dinner as Prakash would be home from work soon. Usha, Prakash, and Kabita made up a small family that lacked nothing in terms of time, money, or love. Even in a country like England, Prakash had a job that matched his education, and Usha also had a decent job. Knowing that Kabita's time would be divided with a second child, they had no plans for another baby.

The sound of the doorbell excited Kabita. She had been silently drawing pictures after school and rushed to the door with her artwork in hand, knowing it was her dad.

"Wow! Did you draw something? Show it to me, my dear," Prakash entered the room eagerly, carrying Kabita. She held her pictures tightly and stared silently at her father, seeming unsure whether to show him the drawings or not.

"Show me, dear! You're a great artist. I love all the pictures you draw," Prakash encouraged, entering the room with Kabita.

Kabita slowly showed her drawings to her father. In one of the drawings, there was a girl, a boy, a woman, and two men in a single frame. Usha and Prakash were both surprised. "Whose family is this, dear?" Usha asked curiously.

"This is Lauren's family," Kabita replied.

"But Lauren's family doesn't have as many people as you've drawn," Prakash laughed.

"Yes, they do. Lauren, Jack, Ben, Suzzana, and Peter," Kabita insisted.

"Dear... Lauren, Jack, Ben, and Suzzana belong to the same family, but Peter belongs to a different family," Prakash corrected the characters in the family frame that Kabita had drawn.

In fact, Peter is Suzzana's ex-husband, who would come every Saturday to pick up his son Ben and daughter Lauren to spend time with them at his own home. This was not an unfamiliar sight in England. Even after separation, fathers, bound by legal and social responsibilities, were seen fulfilling their fatherly duties. They would often bring their young children back to their own home during weekends, take them out, feed them, and then drop them off at their mother's place on Sunday evenings, ready for school on Monday.

Usha brought tea for Prakash. Kabita didn't fully understand what her father said about her drawing. Instead, she randomly drew some more pictures for a while. Suddenly, she remembered something and ran to her parents.

"Mum, why do I only have one daddy? Lauren has two daddies," Kabita innocently asked, sitting on her mother's lap.

Kabita's question caught Usha off guard. She had never thought about it before or imagined that Kabita would be so affected by the neighbours and their activities. Usha and Prakash exchanged blank stares for a moment.

Then, Kabita spoke again. "If I had two daddies like Lauren, I would also get to live in two houses. I could go to another house on Saturdays. Mum, can't I have two daddies?" Kabita's questions were so innocent and straightforward, as if she were asking for two dolls. However, this time, both Usha and Prakash burst into laughter.

Kabita, growing up with the idea of a broken family and with peculiar questions in her mind, left Usha and Prakash perplexed about how to help her comprehend the situation. However, they were reassured that with time, Kabita would come to understand these matters on her own.

***

Shattered Dream

"I will be sharing some bikini photos today and see how many likes they garner," Dilasha said as she carefully selected pictures from a recent photo session with the intention of posting them on Facebook.

"Do you think this one looks fine? It's not too revealing, right?" Dilasha asked Arunima, wanting a second opinion. Arunima hesitated to respond.

"I don't think it's a good idea to post bikini photos," Arunima thought to herself.

Arunima was concerned about Dilasha's changing behaviour and increasing attachment to social media.

"Which bikini pose looks better, the yellow one or the pink one?" Dilasha kept changing her mind and couldn't decide which photos to choose.

"Well, I'm not an expert on bikini photos or social media. Besides, I don't feel comfortable with my own body after giving birth," Arunima replied, looking at her own postpartum body.

Dilasha couldn't fully understand what Arunima meant, except for the last sentence. She wondered if Arunima envied her well-shaped body. With these thoughts in mind, Dilasha closed her laptop and walked into the garden, lost in her own thoughts. She realised the effort she had put into getting her body back in shape after her daughter was born.

After giving birth, Dilasha did gain weight, but it no longer held the same allure it once did. As a result, her husband became less interested in her and started flirting with other women. Dilasha made the decision to move to Arunima's rented apartment with her four-month-old daughter and never looked back at her husband.

During her lonely struggle, she dedicated a year to raising her daughter and, in the process, completely transformed her own body. She spared no expense or time, joining weight loss clubs, fitness centres, and trying expensive diets. This commitment, combined with her newfound confidence and desire for revenge against her unfaithful husband, brought out a radiance in Dilasha that surpassed her former self. People would barely learn that she was a mother of one. Even if someone discovered, they would instead inquire about how she achieved such a model-like figure.

Although Dilasha's body had returned to its original form, she chose to stick to powdered milk for her daughter. She didn't want anything to diminish her beauty. However, Dilasha was far from being an unaffectionate mother. In her thoughts, she loved her daughter even more than before. Her goal was to establish herself as a model in England, aiming to improve her lifestyle. She believed that her sacrifices would greatly benefit her daughter's future.

"Dilasha, the child is crying. Maybe she's hungry," Arunima called out from the living room.

"Did she finish the milk from yesterday?"

"Yes, she already did. Now we need to mix the powdered milk."

"Oh, how forgetful of me. Let me order it online," Dilasha recalled the time when she had spent hours browsing through bikini photos and completely forgotten to order the milk.

Since last week, Dilasha had been purchasing locally sourced breast milk from other mothers. Some people had warned her that it could potentially cause infections in children. However, Dilasha had heard from a Romanian woman she met at work that she had been selling her excess milk, more than what her own child needed. Dilasha saw it as a suitable alternative to powdered milk, thinking to herself, "After all, a mother's milk is a mother's milk." This gave her a sense of satisfaction, believing that she was fulfilling her duty as a mother.

With the cool morning breeze, Dilasha opened her eyes. She had fallen asleep with her mobile phone in her hand, late at night while scrolling through Facebook. As she woke up, her gaze shifted from her surroundings to her mobile phone, and she squinted at the numerous notifications displayed on the screen.

"Two thousand eight hundred likes? Oh my God!" exclaimed Dilasha, sitting up in her bed. Her voice was so sharp and loud that her little daughter woke up startled and began crying.

"Phew! Now I have to comfort her too," Dilasha lifted her daughter, but her mind was consumed with finding out who had written what in the comment section.

"Arunima, hey Arunima! Can you take the baby for a stroll, please?" Dilasha hastily reached for her laptop, eager to see the comments displayed on the larger screen.

"Why are you so anxious and restless about these comments and likes? Are they going to disappear?" Arunima took the baby outside, and Dilasha didn't even spare a glance at her for a moment.

"Oh my god! People are going crazy over here. Just look, Arunima!" Dilasha muttered in excitement, turning her gaze back to the Facebook page open on her laptop.

"Wow! Twenty-seven hundred likes. This is amazing!"

"Twenty-seven hundred likes? Who could have liked my photos?" Dilasha's excitement heightened. Before diving into the comments, she opened the photos she had posted yesterday and smiled. This was the day she had been eagerly waiting for. This was the day she had anticipated.

Dilasha then shifted her attention to the comment section.

"You look like a model."

"Supermodel!"

"Super mom, supermodel looks."

"Teach us how to get a body like a model."

Dilasha's excitement grew as she read the comments. Her heart filled with delight, and her mind buzzed with joy.

"It's a big loss for us. Nepal lost a great modelling talent in you."

As Dilasha gazed at the comments, her heart swelled with emotion upon reading a comment from her old modelling days friend, Anisha. She paused and didn't feel the urge to read any further comments.

With determination, Dilasha whispered, "It's not just about being a model in Nepal; I aspire to become an international model, someone who will be recognised worldwide." She affirmed with renewed vigour, "I will prove myself and showcase my talents to everyone, especially those disgusting Nepalese modelling agencies that once rejected my portfolio." As she reminisced about the past, a soft sigh escaped her lips, each memory evoking a wave of emotions. Two tears gently trickled down her cheeks, overwhelming her with emotion.

"Dilasha, look, the daughter is still unsettled. She hasn't had any milk," Arunima expressed with concern as she approached Dilasha.

"Okay, I will feed her. You must be running late for work as well," Dilasha replied, her voice filled with care and concern.

Scooping her daughter into her arms, Dilasha lifted her tenderly and ventured into the garden, leaving behind the echoes of her daughter's gentle cries. The sweetness of powdered milk no longer enticed her. She had even forgotten to order the Romanian woman's milk, leaving her empty-handed. Dilasha felt conflicted about whether to breastfeed.

"I shouldn't let my spirit falter. It's essential to maintain my body for this journey. Especially as a single mother, my responsibility towards my daughter has multiplied. I must make this sacrifice. It's just a matter of one day. I won't forget to place an order for tomorrow," Dilasha declared with unwavering resolve, determined not to breastfeed her daughter.

With her daughter nestled close, Dilasha fed her the remnants of yesterday's milk and cradled her to bed. She gazed at her daughter for a while and gently kissed her forehead, caressing her hair. It seemed that her daughter had a slight fever, so Dilasha gave her 5ml of Calpol and sent her to sleep.

In Dilasha's world, love may not have been openly expressed, just as she withheld it from her daughter. Yet, amidst the intricate tapestry woven between Dilasha and her daughter, lay countless sacrifices made by her for the sake of her daughter's future. These sacrifices stirred a mix of guilt and strength within Dilasha's heart, forging her determination to face whatever challenges lay ahead.

Dilasha's daughter was peacefully asleep, possibly aided by medication. The moment her daughter surrendered to slumber presented a precious opportunity that Dilasha couldn't afford to miss. She hurried to her laptop, eager for this anticipated respite from the tiring demands of the day. While Facebook likes and comments weren't her ultimate aspirations, they served as milestones on her journey toward self-confidence. The photos from her session were carefully intended for modelling agencies, shaping her portfolio. Each like and comment on her photos was a measure, not of external validation, but of her own path to self-belief.

Dilasha opened Facebook on both her mobile and laptop, the continuous sound of notifications capturing her attention. With limited time since she had given her daughter attention, she couldn't leisurely read through the comments. Leaning forward, she took a deep breath in front of her laptop.

"Three thousand likes! And sixteen hundred comments?" Dilasha wondered as she gazed at herself in the mirror, momentarily captivated by her restored beauty.

With great joy and interest, Dilasha started reading each comment, losing herself in her own colourful world. She hadn't realised she had nurtured this vibrant world within herself. The dream of becoming a model was not just a fantasy; it was her response to her cheating husband who had left her due to her changed appearance. Even if Biraj were to come looking for her, she would never go back to him.

"Dilasha, it's better to live alone than with a partner who doesn't reciprocate your feelings, and only loves your body," Dilasha would read a comment and find herself lost in memories of the past. In the midst of it all, she spent so much time immersed in her dream world that she didn't even have time for lunch.

"Dilasha, hey Dilasha!" Arunima's voice echoed sharply from another room, jolting Dilasha from her reverie.

"Why? Did you return from work early or did you not go at all?" Dilasha inquired.

"Dilasha!" Arunima screamed, causing Dilasha's heart to skip a beat. She quickly rushed towards her daughter's room.

"Hmm, what's the matter?" Her eyes glanced out the window, realising it was already pitch dark outside. Dilasha had been engrossed in Facebook after putting her daughter to sleep during the day, and now it was late in the evening. There was no sound coming from her daughter's room, assuring that she was in a deep sleep. However, it was rare for her daughter to sleep so peacefully.

"Dilasha, the girl is not breathing at all. She passed away. You were supposed to take her to the doctor today..." Arunima's words hit Dilasha hard, especially since her daughter seemed fine during the day. When Arunima, a nurse herself shared the news about her daughter's demise, Dilasha couldn't accept what she was hearing.

"How could this happen?" Dilasha became restless and anxious.

"It might be due to an infection from the milk. Maybe the milk soured in the intense heat. I told you before that this kind of milk doesn't get properly sterilised. And if you had taken her to the hospital on time, she might have been saved. You're in the same position, same room, same corner, same posture as when I left. Perhaps your obsession with an imagined life and spending too much time on Facebook contributed to the unfortunate demise of your daughter," Arunima's words carried anger today. She was frustrated with Dilasha's habit of disregarding her advice, despite her numerous attempts to make her understand. Arunima had stopped advising Dilasha, but today was different. Even though the child was not her own, she cared for Dilasha's daughter more than anything.

The pain of losing her daughter, self-blame, and Arunima's harsh words pushed Dilasha to the brink of despair. She cried, screamed, and cursed herself. The Greenacre neighbourhood resonated with her cries, and even neighbours came to offer their condolences. Arunima had never imagined life taking such an unpredictable and painful turn, not even in her wildest dreams.

Dilasha's Facebook account is now closed. Her thousands of followers have no idea where she is. Only a select few know that Dilasha is facing a ten-year prison sentence for the child's death due to her negligence. Her dream of becoming an international model has been shattered completely. It is unlikely that her Facebook account will ever be reopened.

***

Conflict of Thoughts

Everyone around the world is alive and surviving. Some people appear to be very happy, while others seem quite unhappy. I had a deeply ingrained belief that those who indulged in physical pleasures were much happier than me. Whenever I saw someone in a higher position or driving fancy cars, I imagined they would be happier. I often found myself wishing to be like them. I didn't have anyone who I could truly call my own, whether it be a friend or a sister.

However, Nira was very fond of me, and in her presence, I felt a sense of belonging and affection. I had a special connection with Nira's place, and I sought to discover the true meaning of my solitary life there. I had conflicting thoughts about destiny, sometimes believing in it and sometimes not. These conflicting thoughts were always present within me.

At exactly noon, I pressed the doorbell at Nira's house. I noticed that both of her eyes were red. Since I was used to being alone, the death of Nira's mother didn't affect me much. My own mother had left this world soon after I was born, so I never experienced maternal affection. However, I still felt sorry for Nira.

"Nira, this is how life is! Everyone who comes must eventually leave," I tried to console her. We didn't have any specific topics to discuss, and even if we did, it would only bring up painful memories of her mother. It wasn't worth reopening the wound that had already started to heal. With this in mind, I quickly left.

Nira and I weren't related by blood. The only difference I felt was that she was younger than me. Despite knowing this, I still considered myself the same age as Nira and longed to fulfil my hidden desires through our companionship. She had the freedom to choose her own outfits and was familiar with the latest trends in the market. While I didn't think it was possible for me to own such things, I found satisfaction in seeing Nira enjoy them. It made me feel a sense of ownership indirectly, as she was someone very dear to me.

I went on a three-month trip to Pokhara[21], and during that time, we didn't exchange any letters. I was curious and excited to learn everything about her, just as she was about me. However, whenever she asked me about myself, I tried to steer the conversation elsewhere. She still didn't know that I was an orphan. I started visiting her house frequently after Shanti Didi, who lived downstairs, informed me and I began giving Nira tuition classes. This routine continued, and eventually, I started visiting her on weekends too. That's how our relationship developed.

---

[21] *Pokhara lies approximately 125 miles west of Kathmandu in Nepal.*

Despite the teacher-student dynamic, we managed to avoid formality. I adapted my feelings to match the emotions of young Nira. I wanted to be like her and forget about the age difference between us. Perhaps, being unmarried at the age of thirty-two, I intentionally tried to feel younger. Although thoughts of getting married would occasionally cross my mind, I was always hesitant about it. Like the two faces of a coin, everything has its pros and cons, and in my contemplation, I unintentionally surpassed the age for marriage. I had nothing... no family, no lineage, no wealth, no beauty, nothing. Looking at my sunken hollow eyes, I couldn't help but feel disappointed in myself. Nira had everything that I lacked.

***

Filled with thoughts and a desire to find out how she was, I arrived at her house and pressed the doorbell. An unfamiliar woman opened the door, and I carefully observed her appearance from head to toe. Judging by her unsuccessful attempts to hide her age with cosmetics, I guessed she must be at least thirty-five years old. When I asked about Nira, she simply replied, "This is not Nira's house," and abruptly shut the door, leaving me surprised.

How could I believe it wasn't Nira's house? I was familiar with every item and corner of that house. Then, I suddenly remembered the blurry image of a lady often riding pillion on Nira's father's motorcycle. However, I wasn't entirely sure about my memory. With these thoughts occupying my mind, I left. On my way, I ran into Harke and couldn't contain my curiosity any longer. I blurted out, "Where is Nira? Who was that woman?"

"Nira is currently staying at her aunt's place. She won't come back... She doesn't want to be here anymore. Her father intended to arrange a marriage for her, so she left the house," Harke explained, his eyes brimming with tears. Curiosity got the better of me, and I asked, "Who is the woman inside the house?"

"Who else? The boss's new wife! I don't want to stay here either. Every day, I receive scoldings from the boss for falsely accusing me of not serving his mistress adequately."

Poor Harke! He had been working as a domestic help in that house since Nira's birth, taking care of her and providing her love throughout her childhood. However, Nira decided to leave the house and move to her aunt's place. Her aunt, her father's only sister, had chosen to remain unmarried, seeing marriage as an unnecessary social obligation. I couldn't help but worry about whether Nira would be able to cope in her new environment. She was the only daughter of a doctor mother and a businessman father.

Nira's situation made me feel anxious. The harsh reality hit me harder than it did Nira. Like her, I also had my own desires, but most of them remained unfulfilled. I wasn't interested in the marriage proposal from Shanti Didi. I longed for a life of freedom. To achieve that, I had to either live unmarried like Nira's aunt or risk ending up like Nira's shattered family. Although I was an orphan, I was someone who sought to define my own existence. I couldn't bear the thought of being confined within the four walls of a house like a typical woman. I had the courage to shoulder the responsibilities of both the inside and outside of the house. Would this path lead me to a fate similar to Nira's mother?

Whenever I saw Nira's mother, I wondered what it would be like to become a doctor. However, the house I considered a sanctuary turned out to be hollow on the inside. Men in our society often restrict women's freedom, while women yearn for independence. This conflict of thoughts has plagued this century. Even as a doctor, what could Nira's mother do? The demands of emergencies, night duties, and her responsibilities caused headaches for Nira's father. They had been contemplating a divorce, but unfortunately, Nira's mother lost her battle with cancer before they could proceed.

I desired freedom, yet I also yearned to escape from that very freedom. I was caught in a state of confusion. Would society allow Nira to confidently stride forward? Wasn't marriage considered a necessary milestone in the later stages of life? In Nepal, it was still common to blame and shame unmarried women. Despite reaching that stage myself, I hadn't been able to find a life partner.

The absence of love weighed heavily on my mind, with no one to share my sorrows. Nira was there, but she also seemed to envision a challenging and gloomy future for me. Sometimes, when she asked why I wasn't married, I would be startled and at a loss for words. I feared that after marriage, the absence of love I experienced before might become even more pronounced. All I wished for was a life that wouldn't shatter after marriage. When I observed Nira's family, I admired her mother's values and aspired to be like her. However, the interpretation I had made turned out to be completely opposite. Despite being an ideal wife, she had to endure numerous insults from her husband.

Nira's mother died in pain, and Nira left home. In due course, her father remarried. Life, burdened by the weight of loneliness, dreamt of a bright future ahead, but all in vain. I had been alone since birth. How much longer could I continue like this? From being called Rashmi to Rashmi Didi[22], and now Rashmi Aunty by some young girls, life had taken its course. Should I escape from men, or should I fight? I found myself trapped in these thoughts, feeling lost. In this manner, the window for my marriage seemed to fade away, slipping through the fingers of time.

***

[22] *Elder sister*

The Writer's Story

Purnima's life was truly larger than life. She had a name that matched her lifestyle, which was as luminous as a full moon. Initially, she worked as a teacher but eventually left her job to pursue her passion for literature and writing. She devoted herself to keenly observing the behaviours of those around her and skilfully incorporating certain characters and elements into her stories, adding a touch of artistic brilliance. This was her unique talent.

Sometimes, I would come across fragments of myself in her stories, but understanding Purnima proved challenging, both within and outside her narratives. I speculated that perhaps writers may depict themselves and their personalities in such a manner, although I could be mistaken. Nevertheless, Purnima's presence in my life made me believe in this idea.

I was Purnima's closest friend, and I witnessed her countless stories being neglected and left unpublished. I longed for her stories to come alive and reach a wide audience. Yet, it wasn't just about crafting exceptional stories; it was also about the challenge of capturing the attention of editors in a sea of writers and truly touching people's hearts. Perhaps that's one of the reasons why her beautifully written stories managed to make it to publishing houses but never made it to print.

When I compared her stories to those of other published authors, I found Purnima's work to be of equal quality, if not better. It bewildered me that some of these magazines relied solely on the reputation of mediocre authors whose stories lacked substance. I often pondered why Purnima's stories couldn't find a place in those publications. The concept of name and reputation itself is strange. This was Purnima, the writer who remained obscured, yet I continued to be her devoted admirer.

During our teenage days, I took Purnima to my uncle Laxman's publishing house. I accompanied her as she sought solace from the drafts of her stories that struggled within the pages of her notebook. With hope in my heart, I approached Uncle Laxman, presenting him with the entire collection of her written stories. I had anticipated his support, but my hopes were dashed. Uncle Laxman advised us to leave the stories in his office, and we returned home after submitting them. How could I not trust him? He was not only my uncle but also the Chief Editor of a weekly magazine.

However, it was my mistake to have faith in the strength of our relationship and the integrity of his profession. To my dismay, her stories were published in the following weeks, but all under my uncle's name. Witnessing Purnima's anguish and tears of despair in the days that followed shattered my heart. I saw her spirit wither away within the confines of her room, as if she was slowly dying with every passing moment. I found myself consumed by regret, but I was utterly powerless. In that state of helplessness, I even confronted my uncle in a desperate attempt to rectify the situation, but it proved futile. In the face of his advanced age, his printing press, his reputation, and the influence of his pen, our sorrowful pleas and Purnima's writing held no sway.

Following Uncle Laxman's betrayal, Purnima locked away her own creations within the depths of her heart, as if they were sentenced to a lifetime of imprisonment. Her stories became entangled within the intricate maze of her mind. This was the nature of Purnima—whenever she faced hardships, her pen would cease to move. I had heard that writers often express their pain and emotions through their words, but Purnima seemed to be an exception. After all, which scripture or book could fully capture the complexities of an individual's mindset or unique behaviour?

Despite being a student of psychology, I struggled to fully comprehend her inner world. Whenever Purnima encountered a problem, she would take her time to navigate through the accompanying pain, gradually finding her way back to her path. If she had found a reputable publishing agency, she would have already established herself as a remarkable writer. Fate also plays a significant role, as one's desires are not easily granted. It was through her stories that I contemplated the profound impact that the support or absence thereof from time can have. Purnima's stories taught me about the challenges of surviving in society when one struggles to adapt to the ever-changing tides of time and circumstances.

Time raced on at its own pace. Purnima's usually active pen had come to a halt here. On the other hand, my own pen would often stumble, falter, and wander aimlessly. I lacked the ability to unleash my imagination and allow my words to soar. Perhaps that was my weakness. The words I wrote never blossomed into proper literature, and I deemed them far from being literary. As a result, I would secretly tear apart and discard the pages scribbled with my writing, a habit I had developed since childhood. I never allowed even the slightest hint of this to reach Purnima or any of my family members. However, as a reader, I excelled. I possessed the patience required of a reader, and thus, Purnima never felt the absence of vast readership after that incident. She considered her stories complete once I had immersed myself in them. In fact, Purnima had an inexplicable reliance on me.

Time is an ever-changing force, and embracing change is an inevitable truth that we cannot avoid. As a student of psychology, I recognised that delving into literature was a departure from the structured research papers I was accustomed to. Therefore, I suppressed my desires and aspirations, choosing to proceed at my own pace. I buried the longing within the recesses of my heart, convincing myself that becoming a writer was merely a passing interest.

Perhaps it was Purnima's influence that shaped this mindset within me. The emotional weight carried by the random words I would haphazardly scribble held no true essence compared to Purnima's refined stories. I believed they deserved to be discarded, and without hesitation, I would write and discard them without anyone's notice.

Purnima incorporated many aspects of my life into her stories, yet I never revealed this hidden facet of my life to my dearest friend. It is often said that no one in the world truly knows everything about another person. At times, I even questioned whether I truly knew myself.

Time and circumstances can create distance between individuals and the situations they find themselves in. As life took a turn, I found myself growing apart from Purnima. Moreover, Manish's evident fondness for her added to my discomfort. After Manish and I got married, he would often share his writings with me, and some of his stories were even published. He would eagerly ask me to read them. Such was the rhythm of my life.

My adolescent years were spent immersed in Purnima's stories, but now, in my leisure time, I found myself engrossed in Manish's writings. However, regardless of whether they were published or not, Manish's stories never resonated with me in the same way that Purnima's did. Expressing this to Manish would risk breaking his heart, but keeping it unsaid would mean living with the guilt of deceiving myself. So, I resorted to a small deception, simply to encourage him and maintain his happiness.

My life had become a twisted fate, caught between two opposing forces. On one side were Purnima's stories, and on the other were Manish's writings. Amidst it all, I would occasionally contemplate my own existence and sense of self. Just as I used to hide my writings from Purnima and my family members in the past, I continued to do so even after marrying Manish. I would scribble and discard my writings without anyone's knowledge. Manish never had the slightest inkling about this, and neither did he make any effort to inquire. Nor did I feel the need to reveal this hidden aspect of myself.

Purnima would visit my house just as she visited my parents' home when we were young. I never considered myself separate from her. However, after the birth of my son, I found myself struggling to find time to read both Manish and Purnima's stories. Reading stories became just one of many competing priorities in my life, and fulfilling those responsibilities consumed most of my time, leaving little room for reading.

There were moments when I contemplated stringing together the words from my heap of research papers and presenting them as a literary work. However, throughout my life, I never felt a deep connection with my own words or the courage to share them. They lacked the liveliness and intrigue present in the characters of Purnima and Manish's stories. I was trapped in the labyrinth of time constraints.

Despite my own challenges, Purnima and Manish continued to share their stories with each other. Sometimes, I expressed regret for not being able to participate in those gatherings and promised to catch up on all the stories once our child grew older.

It was Manish who gradually consoled and encouraged Purnima, emphasising the need for her stories to be published. I, too, agreed with Manish, but after the betrayal from Uncle Laxman, I felt that Purnima had stopped listening to me. Unbeknownst to her, Manish had submitted the stories she had given him to read for publication. Finally, Purnima's stories were published— perhaps it was her fate this time, or maybe her stories had become even more refined than before. The task that I couldn't accomplish in ten years, Manish achieved in just a few months.

Time slipped away, bringing together two significant characters in my life—Manish and Purnima—who complemented each other by sharing and appreciating each other's works. I found myself unable to intervene in any way. My heart, as a woman, felt constricted within these circumstances, yet I remained silent, with only a few scattered words fluttering between the pages of my notebook. They engaged in conversations about literature, the publishing process, and shared their respective works. Yet, how narrow-minded I was. On one side, I had a childhood friend, and on the other side, a husband with whom I had exchanged vows for a lifetime.

Over time, I began to exert control over my perceived narrow-mindedness, although there was little else I could do. My mind, however, remained entangled between these two individuals, wondering how the relationships closest to me turned a blind eye to the situation I was in. Whenever Purnima called on the landline, my heart would skip a beat, and my hands trembled, and legs shook.

But now, those calls were limited to Manish's mobile phone. I couldn't wholeheartedly accept the hours they spent conversing under the guise of literary discussions. At times, I wondered if they were writers or the antagonistic characters in the story of my own downfall. My heart grew weary, yet these literary souls never delved into my exhausted heart or made any effort to understand. It seemed that one day, these writers would empty the tales of my own life under the pretext of sharing stories.

Disheartened by the changes brought about by their lifestyles, I felt that the character 'Me' no longer fit into the narratives of these two writers. Despite my background in psychological research, I struggled to comprehend the mindset of these authors at this turning point in life. Consequently, I made the decision to distance myself from both of them without hesitation. I believed it was the only remedy for the daily wounds inflicted upon me.

Surprisingly, whatever I had asked of Manish, he easily granted, as if it was what he truly desired as well—separation from me. I felt that Purnima had taken my place in his life. Through her stories, Purnima had brought an end to my own story, and it felt more than just the conclusion of a narrative—it marked the end of a marriage, trust, and belief. It was better to put an end to the story once and for all, rather than living with the pain like a scorching iron rod pressed against my skin. It was preferable to die once than to experience repeated deaths. Therefore, I had no regrets about the decision I had made. However, Manish never accepted this reality, nor did Purnima. Yet, I believed that I understood the psychology of human beings. How could I ignore the knowledge I had acquired through reading, observing, and experiencing?

As time went by, I found myself engrossed in taking care of my son and focusing on my job, completely unaware that five years had slipped away. In the midst of this busy life, my book titled 'Depression and Divorcees' was published, and with its release, I started receiving an influx of phone calls, emails, and congratulatory messages. Amongst the sea of notifications, one email stood out—a lengthy message from Purnima. As I read through the contents of her email, it left a profound impact on me.

"Mamta, first and foremost, congratulations on the success of your book. It seems to have caused quite a stir in the market. However, Mamta, you need to understand that the buzz is not solely about your achievements, but rather about the exposure of our personal lives, including yours, Manish's, and mine. It seems you have been enticed by the trend of gaining fame by tarnishing others' reputations. Throughout your life, you have confined yourself within the boundaries of stubbornness and self-will, and within that same confinement, you have inflicted pain upon both me and Manish.

The relationship between Manish and me was quite different from what you seemed to see. Perhaps only a like-minded author who can weave stories, transforming mere imagination into a narrative, can truly grasp it. Just as you used to comment on how I shaped the nature of my characters based on the people around me, writers often incorporate elements of themselves and their surroundings into their scattered pieces of imagination. Unlike you, I never wrote a story where you were the central character. Even if fragments of your presence appeared here and there, the character would be concealed under a pseudonym. This ensured that readers, despite searching for resemblances in real life, could never identify the true person behind the portrayal.

But I am astounded... why did you choose to present my life so openly in the market? I have no answer to this, except that perhaps it was your way of garnering sympathy and achieving cheap popularity. Do you realise, Mamta, that I write stories as a mere hobby, crafting characters and narratives? On the other hand, you misused your pen by assassinating the characters of both Manish and me, fabricating your own narratives, and using them as a means to establish yourself as a great psychological writer in the market. I am unsure if my words will affect you in any way, but Manish, trapped and shattered by your actions, has left his world, and perhaps his soul will never forgive you."

Upon reading Purnima's email, a sense of emptiness washed over me. The final sentence of her message struck a deep chord within me, leaving me profoundly unsettled. It was in the midst of our separation that Manish tragically passed away, just two years later, in a sudden and unforeseen road accident. Yet, Purnima's accusation had once again pierced through my heart. She managed to shatter me anew, much like she had shattered the fragments of my married life. In my perspective of events, I viewed her as the instigator, the one at fault. However, in her narrative, the blame fell upon me.

Purnima's words had once again cast a shadow of inadequacy over my present life. I had embarked on fulfilling her childhood dream of becoming a renowned writer, but it felt futile to believe that only visionaries had the privilege of living their dreams. Life's twists and turns constantly reshuffle the tables, causing some dreams to crumble while new ones emerge. In the midst of it all, writers and storytellers are born. Some hone their writing skills over time, while others are compelled by the pressures of life to become writers. In my case, time's relentless pressure had propelled the writer within me into the hands of readers.

Perhaps my readers would understand my perspective, but the eyes and minds of writers like Purnima, who drew inspiration from fragments of people's lives for their stories, had closed themselves off to me. In my book, I never mentioned Purnima's name or Manish's name. In truth, I had bared my own life to provide momentum and inspiration to countless friends who, like me, had endured betrayal from their life partners and had wrestled with depression and post-traumatic stress disorder (PTSD). If someone is connected to my life, can I not write about the person? Where is the justice in that?

Purnima may have seen herself reflected in the character depicted in my book, but she failed to realise that her character and persona remained nameless. Readers would recognise her merely as one of the women who traversed the ups and downs of my life, not as Purnima. I could barely comprehend the mindset of a writer like her. Nonetheless, her accusations held no weight in my life today. Hence, I felt no compulsion to write a clarifying response to her email.

***

The Journal of an Unsettled Mind

As per the calendar, today is 25th June 2017. I have decided to start keeping a personal diary from today onwards. I am unsure whether this journal will serve as a mere record or an attempt to document significant events in my life. Unlike most diaries that are updated daily, my pen has its own rhythm and sometimes even races across the pages. This pen seems to have a mind of its own, perhaps a touch stubborn or independent. I must admit, I am not particularly enthusiastic about writing a diary, but there are moments in life when loneliness creeps in, and you find solace in the company of pen and notebook. Despite having numerous friends on social media, their presence doesn't make much of a difference, merely superficial connections. The only place where I can pour out my true anguish is within the pages of this diary. All other emotions are filtered and expressed based on the strength and depth of my connections with others.

30 June 2017

As I flip through the pages of my diary today, my pen traces back to my blissful past. It's strange how certain moments of joy can eventually cause pain. After all, why would one feel saddened when reminiscing about joyful times? However, like everyone else, I am also a sensitive person. I too have a past that brimmed with happiness. Whenever I recall those cherished days, they unfold before me like a delightful scene from a movie. It was during those golden days that Urmila and I embarked on our own story.

Urmila is a nurse by profession and also my beloved wife. We entered the sacred bond of marriage eight years ago, filled with boundless love and understanding. Our relationship evolved from two years of dating to a marriage, and our life together was progressing smoothly. I made sure never to betray Urmila's trust in me, accepting her wishes wholeheartedly. She was an educated and understanding wife.

However, my mother, who considered herself modern and open-minded, and granted her daughter the same freedom as her sons, struggled to extend that same open-mindedness to her daughter-in-law. While she showered Urmila with love, she always found something to criticise regarding the level of dedication and special treatment she expected from a daughter-in-law. I found myself constantly mediating conflicts between my mother and Urmila, striving to maintain a fair balance, and I never regretted doing so. I believed it was a common experience for married men and mostly remained silent. Such was the nature of my life—sometimes leaning towards my mother, sometimes towards my wife. The responsibility was weighty, requiring constant equilibrium, which made me remain vigilant most of the time.

In our two years of married life, Urmila spared no effort in fulfilling the role of an ideal wife. She was calm and uncomplicated, and I considered myself fortunate to have her as my wife. However, today she left for work without even bidding me goodbye as usual. This left me feeling disheartened. Time is ever-changing, and that is undeniable, but Urmila's behaviour, of late, has deeply saddened me. Maybe she doesn't realise the impact it has on me.

1 July 2017

Today, I find myself vividly reminiscing about the busy eventful nature of my past work. Perhaps it was triggered by the news I've been closely following online. The images of protests and rallies by human rights activists, demanding justice for the murder of Manamaya and the display of placards and demonstrations in Maitighar[23], have brought back memories from my own past.

I used to work as a Human Rights Officer for a non-governmental organisation in Nepal. I can still recall those days when I actively took part in demonstrations and rallies, holding placards and exerting pressure through loud slogans, even with an empty stomach. We would gather in front of Singha Durbar[24] or at Maitighar Mandala, fervently advocating against violence towards women. At times, I

---

[23] *Maitighar, an iconic public space located in the heart of Kathmandu, is a significant venue for protests and demonstrations in Nepal.*
[24] *Singha Durbar, situated in Kathmandu, serves as the official seat of the government of Nepal.*

would stumble upon interviews of myself published in magazines and newspapers, where some praised my efforts while others extended their best wishes. Many believed that I would make significant contributions to the field of women's rights in Nepal.

As time passed, my self-confidence grew, and I remained determined to continue my work. However, after getting married, pursuing both of our dreams together became quite challenging. It wasn't easy to compromise solely on one's aspirations, and that became the central issue.

However, as I look back now, I realise that Urmila's dreams were equally valid. After working diligently as a nurse at Bir Hospital for four years, she gained valuable experience and expertise in her field. Urmila possessed exceptional capabilities, and her determination led her to succeed in whatever she pursued. I also considered myself incredibly fortunate. I had no grievances or complaints regarding my wife, as there was never a need for any.

However, in recent times I find myself increasingly concerned and disheartened by Urmila's changing behaviour. Today, she arrived home at 9 p.m., informing me via a text message that she had a surprise dinner party with friends. I took care of Prawesh and Sarwesh, putting them to bed. With Urmila absent, I didn't have the appetite to eat, so I didn't bother cooking anything. When Urmila returned, she went straight to sleep without inquiring about my dinner, as expected. Rather than engaging in conversation with Urmila, who lay beside me, I find myself pouring out my thoughts with a pen and a notebook. What kind of life is this…

10 July 2017

A video posted on Facebook by Amit Baskota, a former colleague from Nepal, unexpectedly triggered a flood of memories from the past. His recent interview on Kantipur TV deeply touched me. Amit, who held a similar position as an "Officer" like me, is now leading a non-governmental organisation. In his interview, he mentioned my name as a source of inspiration for his journey into the field of human rights.

While I am happy for my friends' progress, it also leads me to question myself about my own identity and purpose. I often ponder the mistakes I may have made by choosing to settle abroad. I haven't been able to find a definitive answer. Has my identity become solely defined by my red UK passport? This question haunts me nowadays. Moreover, obtaining this red passport wasn't a personal desire, but rather a necessity. I had already obtained a permanent residency visa, which allowed me to stay indefinitely in the UK. However, due to Urmila's aspiration to travel the world, the complications of obtaining visas through a Nepali passport, and the petty quarrels we had associated with that, we decided to obtain British citizenship.

On the day I received this passport, Urmila tightly hugged me, expressing her immense happiness. That was the only achievement this passport brought me. Undoubtedly, it makes international travel more convenient, but it has distanced me from my love for the green passport of Nepal. Regardless of how much I try to identify myself as a Nepali at heart, I have already become a British citizen.

What Urmila viewed as a matter of pride, for me, has become a source of pain.

5 August 2017

London, the bustling city, emanates such vibrancy and energy. Yet, amidst all the liveliness, I find myself growing increasingly lonely within its confines. It seems as though emptiness has taken residence in my mind. There are moments when frustration overwhelms me, and I find myself questioning why I chose to settle abroad. I yearn for happiness, yet I am perplexed as to how to attain it.

Urmila is on duty. I am preparing meals after putting our sons, Prawesh and Sarwesh, to bed. It's the same lentils, rice, vegetables, and meat—but today, I'm putting in extra effort to ensure a delicious meal as Urmila has an appetite for tasty food. Although she is a skilled cook herself, the responsibility of managing the household has fallen on me.

In this country, there is no strict division of labour based on gender unlike in Nepal. We manage our household tasks based on the time available to us, following a particular schedule. I have no objections to this arrangement. Even in Nepal, I used to assist Urmila with her chores discreetly, despite my mother's disapproval. Occasionally, my mother would express her discontent, but I chose to ignore her and continue supporting Urmila. I believed that if, as a human rights activist, I couldn't bring about change within myself, how could I expect society to change? It brought me joy to see my determination and vision in action.

Some of my colleagues confined their principles of human and women's rights to mere documents. Witnessing their behaviour in their own households, I felt they were somewhat disconnected from their principles. However, I respected their personal lives and refrained from interfering.

Once, when I attempted to address the unjust behaviour of my close friend Mahesh towards his wife, he distanced himself from me. As a result, I restricted my principles to the workplace and my own home, finding contentment in that. Transforming at least my own household was an achievement for me. Hence, my efforts were focused on resolving the conflicts between my mother's beliefs and Urmila's desires and dreams.

15 August 2017

Today is Urmila's birthday. She returned from work with happiness. However, it seems that expressing my love for her at home is not enough to make her truly happy. She remains doubtful unless I demonstrate it on social media. I noticed the joy and excitement on Urmila's face when she arrived home today, and it became clear that she had checked her Facebook, as I spared no effort in praising her in my Facebook post. I shared a picture of our trip to Switzerland and expressed how fortunate and happy I feel to have a wife like her. She couldn't be happier.

Urmila's happiness brings me happiness as well, but it also triggers a sense of fear within me. The happier she becomes, the more alcohol she consumes. And with each glass, her behaviour tends to become more volatile. I failed to realise that Urmila had undergone significant changes over time.

She started drinking in the company of her friends only after we moved to the UK. Despite my attempts to address her drinking habit, she has not shown any signs of change. When she becomes intoxicated, she directs abusive language and verbal profanity towards me. I am exhausted from dealing with Urmila's behaviour when she's drunk. While it's not uncommon to face verbal abuse during arguments, it becomes unbearable when she throws her drink at me. It's difficult to find someone who would believe this situation, and it feels embarrassing to share that I, as a man, am a victim of abuse from a woman. Moreover, being an advocate for human rights, I strive to handle the situation.

I often spend my days contemplating whether Urmila's behaviour can be corrected through my love, understanding, and affection. In moments of anger, she even threatens to leave me, but I have never considered destroying our family life. Instead, I have entrusted Urmila's recovery to the hands of time.

20 August 2017

Today, I feel physically weak. My mental strength has also significantly declined over the years. I had been struggling to find a suitable job in the UK, and after numerous challenges, I finally secured a part-time job. However, I had to leave that job after our son, Prawesh, was born, which added to my difficulties. While Urmila easily found a job during her nursing placement, my work and studies were not valued as much here. Additionally, I also had concerns about who would take care of our son. It didn't seem wise to spend more money on childcare than what I earned. Consequently, we agreed that I would take care of the household responsibilities while Urmila worked outside. It wasn't just a decision but rather a necessary choice forced upon us by the circumstances. In plain words, I have become a "house husband" for now.

Unfortunately, my mother does not appreciate this decision and fails to understand our arrangement. She frequently asks me about my day on the phone, and I try to divert the conversation by mentioning that I have been spending most of my time playing with our son. After Prawesh was born, my mother stayed with us in London for a few months and she disapproved of me doing household chores like cooking and cleaning. She was astonished to see me taking care of the kids and managing the household. Personally, I have no complaints about this situation. There is no book in the world that dictates specific gender roles for work. I have always opposed such narrow-minded ideologies and fought for women's rights in Nepal. I used to discuss principles, deliver speeches, and give interviews on this topic.

However, I truly faced the practical implications of these ideas only when I came to the UK. At times, I even questioned myself if I was being a hypocritical advocate for women's rights, but I never allowed myself to fail during those challenging moments. Perhaps it is my positive thinking that has helped me stay strong in difficult situations. I remain slightly optimistic that once Prawesh grows up, I will have the opportunity to return to university and secure a good job.

25 August 2017

Do women truly possess inherent weakness? Last night, Urmila, in a drunken state, slapped me twice. It never occurred to me that women are the weaker sex. Perhaps, on a physical level, they might be slightly weaker due to natural differences. However, living with Urmila has shattered even that belief.

In the past, she was incredibly active and excelled in sports. Her confidence is what initially attracted me to her. Urmila had already achieved the level of empowerment I envisioned for women. Her self-assurance didn't require speeches or ideological discussions from a women's rights activist like myself. However, the responsibility of managing the household, caring for the children, and keeping the wheels of life turning has fallen solely upon me.

In Nepal, many of my articles and interviews shed light on the burden of domestic chores on women, often disregarded as non-work. I voiced concerns about women being weighed down by the dual roles of homemaker and breadwinner, shedding light on the issue of domestic violence stemming from such dynamics. But now, the tables have turned.

However, my oppressed mind, or simply put, my male mind, shaped by societal expectations, laments the situation. During petty arguments with Urmila, I never tried to argue back. No matter how heated the argument became, I never laid a hand on her. This stance is rooted in my deeply ingrained principles.

When my father raised his hand against my mother, she left home and disappeared with me one day. Neither my father searched for us nor did my mother consider returning. That incident was the reason behind the promise my mother asked me to make when I was young. I was content because that promise led me to choose a career that significantly boosted my confidence.

Today, certain past events attempt to resurface in my mind, but the sound of Prawesh crying compels me to close the diary. If time favoured, I may revisit the joys of my past and bring them into the present.

1 September 2017

Today marks our 9th wedding anniversary.

A week ago, I had already prepared a beautiful photo of Urmila and me together, along with a status to post on Facebook for this special occasion. I even searched on Google for ideas on what to write. Sometimes, I feel that social media has complicated matters for people like me who prefer expressing themselves offline. However, posting on Facebook has become necessary to ensure Urmila's happiness and contentment. Regardless of how many gifts I give or how many heartfelt words of love I express, Urmila won't feel completely satisfied unless a Facebook status is shared.

To commemorate our wedding anniversary, I posted a heartfelt Facebook status accompanied by a photo of Urmila and me, expressing how fortunate I am to have her as my wife. Later that evening, while I was occupied with the usual routine of putting our boys to bed and watching TV, I received a call from Rima, one of Urmila's friends. I woke the boys up, and brought them along in the car to go and pick up Urmila.

It turned out that Urmila and her colleagues were at a pub, celebrating one of her coworker's birthday named Jack. They had been enjoying themselves, but Urmila had consumed a significant number of drinks and was now completely intoxicated. Inside, I was seething with anger and had the urge to slap her, but despite the intense emotions, I refrained from resorting to violence. When we arrived home, Urmila collapsed onto the sofa, completely worn out.

"Urmila, this is unacceptable! Please control yourself," I said, barely able to contain my frustration. Without missing a beat, she fired back, saying, "It's not like I get drunk every day. And when I do, I pay for it with my own money, not yours."

I tried to maintain a calm tone as I responded, "Weren't you aware that I was waiting for you to cut the cake?" Hoping for some affectionate words from Urmila on our anniversary, I was met with the opposite as she replied, "I know! I didn't realise how quickly time passed while I was with my friends."

I had reached my limit of tolerance. It's not that I had never been angry before. The pressures of managing the household and taking care of the kids had often tested my patience. But this time, I couldn't remain silent any longer. I raised my voice and yelled, "Don't you realise you are a mother of two? You have a responsibility towards them too."

In the midst of the conversation, Urmila abruptly exclaimed, "Do you have any idea how challenging it is to earn a living in the UK? The work pressure is overwhelming. It's not as simple as staying at home, cooking meals, and taking care of the kids."

Honestly, I was taken aback by Urmila's response. I was left speechless, struggling to find the right words to reply. The decision for me to stay at home and look after the children was something we had agreed upon mutually. While I could have pursued a part-time job, I chose to focus on enhancing my skills during my spare time, rather than solely prioritising earning money. Working at places like McDonald's or Pizza Hut wouldn't satisfy my aspirations. While I have contemplated returning to Nepal on numerous occasions, I couldn't bring myself to leave Urmila alone and live separately from our family. That was the primary issue at hand.

The harsh reality is that being financially dependent on others can subject a person to ridicule and humiliation in life. I have come to realise this now. It brings to mind all the women, who like me single-handedly manage their homes and children. In this country, I may seem insignificant to others, and this realisation brings tears to my eyes. However, it seems that Urmila has forgotten the crucial role both wheels play in propelling the chariot of life forward.

Urmila, completely intoxicated, remained sprawled on the sofa ever since I brought her home. She was mumbling incoherently. Despite my attempts to control her, I couldn't lift her to take her to bed. Instead, I contemplated gently moving her, slowly dragging her towards the bedroom. Meanwhile, Urmila continued her drunken ramblings.

"Jack, I can't bear to live without you... We can't remain apart. Sarwesh has grown up a bit, but Prawesh is still an infant. You don't have time to take care of him. Jack, will you wait for me?" Urmila embraced me, mistaking me for Jack. "Tell me, Jack, please tell me."

In that moment, it felt as if my entire world had crumbled. It had only been two years since Jack had started working at the London Hospital, where Urmila was also employed. I vividly recall the day when I visited the hospital to meet Urmila, and that's when she introduced me to Jack. It was likely Jack's first week on the job.

Life can be incredibly painful. Today, it became evident that my purpose in life is solely confined to raising our children, particularly Prawesh. It seems like a practical decision and a smart financial move for Urmila to have me take care of our kids instead of sending them to costly childcare facilities. Sarwesh, who is already eight years old, has started attending school, which means he no longer requires childcare services.

During the initial years of our life in the UK, Urmila faced immense pressures from work, placements, and studies. In the same way as now, for three years, I dedicated my efforts to raising Sarwesh. In my fervour of advocating for women's rights, I overlooked my own fundamental human rights. I went beyond the boundaries of trust to help Urmila achieve her dreams, often neglecting my own existence. That's why I never looked at Urmila with suspicion, even when her colleague Jack frequently called and messaged her.

However, today, my mind is unsettled, and my heart aches with the realisation that I hold no place in Urmila's life. As I glance at my mobile phone, Facebook remains open, flooded with notifications. The comments overflow with phrases like "Lovely Couple" and "Best Couple". Nevertheless, I am merely a silent observer, my life suspended at this critical juncture.

Urmila remains partially unconscious, repeatedly mistaking me for Jack as she embraces me. I am uncertain about what the future holds for our relationship. The pages of my diary stare back at me, but my pen struggles to move.

***

Translator's Note

"Translation is like venturing into uncharted waters, attempting to navigate the vast depths of language and culture with only a compass of words. The slightest miscalculation can result in linguistic shipwrecks or lost meanings."

My primary goal has been to capture the core essence of each story and present it in a manner that deeply resonates with English-speaking readers. These stories, set against the backdrop of the plights faced by the Nepali community across various geographies, delve into a wide array of subjects such as love, loss, exploitation, societal prospects, identity crises, and personal growth. I have taken utmost care to maintain the authentic voice and emotional depth of each narrative, allowing readers to immerse themselves fully in the rich tapestry of Sangita's words.

This collection provides a profound insight into the intricacies of human connections and the challenges encountered by individuals in diverse cultural and societal settings. The stories consistently explore themes of yearning, transformation, and self-exploration, encouraging introspection about one's own life experiences. Simply put, this collection offers a poignant portrayal of the complex emotional landscape of people in Nepal and the Nepali diaspora.

Throughout the translation process, I have remained sincere in preserving the cultural subtleties and ensuring that the stories maintain the necessary authenticity and depth. Nonetheless, if any discrepancies have managed to slip in despite my unwavering efforts, I wholeheartedly accept responsibility and assure you of being watchful in the future.

I am deeply thankful to Dr. Sangita Swechcha for granting me the opportunity to translate her esteemed collection. I also extend my sincere appreciation to Dr. Siân Harris for her invaluable comments on the translated stories. Additionally, I am grateful to Book Hill Int'l for providing us with a larger platform to share these bittersweet stories with a broader audience.

Translating these stories has been an incredible opportunity for me to explore the complexities of each narrative and convey the desired emotions and messages articulately. I hope that these stories will truly touch your hearts and spark meaningful conversations about the shared human experience, just as they did for me.

- Jayant Sharma
Emal: jayant.catchme@gmail.com

About the Translator

Jayant Sharma is a writer, editor, and literary translator who mainly works in the Nepali-English language pair. With over two dozen translated literary works, he advocates for the global recognition of Nepali literature. He served as the executive editor of SATHI, an English literary magazine that actively promotes Nepali literature through translations, and is the founder of translateNEPAL, an initiative that highlights Nepal's literary presence on the global stage.

Jayant makes regular contributions to South-Asian journals on topics related to Nepali arts, culture, and literature. He is also the author of 'To Whom It May Concern,' a poetry collection published in Australia.

Beyond his literary pursuits, he is a gifted lyricist and musician, crafting melodies for Nepali movies and artists. With a professional background in computer engineering, he adeptly navigates between the realms of technology and creative arts, seamlessly merging the two worlds.

About the Author

Sangita Swechcha is a Nepali writer based in England. Her poems, stories, and articles have been published in various literary sites and international journals.

Sangita's remarkable journey as a writer started with the publication of her debut novel 'Pakhalieko Siundo' (in Nepali) when she was 18. The novel has recently been republished with a new title named 'Seto Siundo'. The novel is about female tolerance for pain and suffering. It also tells the story of the trafficking of girls and women in Nepal. Her collection of short stories 'Gulafsangako

Prem', published in 2019, has now been translated as 'Rose's Odyssey: Tales of love and loss'. Her upcoming novel, 'A Quest for Bonding', focuses on women's psychology, sexuality, health issues, body image, social stigma as well as acceptance.

Sangita served as the Guest Editor for Nepali literature month organised by Global Literature in Libraries initiatives (GLLI) in the USA in 2019, bringing Nepali literature to a global audience. This culminated in the creation of 'The Himalayan Sunrise', edited by Sangita Swechcha and Karen Van Drie. Additionally, with Andrée Roby, she curated 'A Glimpse Into My Country: A collection of international short stories,' capturing narratives from Africa to Asia and Europe. The book has recently been listed as the text book at the University of California, Irvin (UCI).

A Contributing Author at the 'Global Voices' and the Founder of Book Hill International, Sangita is also a literary campaigner who is raising a voice to bring Nepali literature to the world stage. Recognised for her literary contributions, she has recently been honoured with the 'Nawaratna Nari Award' by the International Nepali Literary Society (INLS).

Sangita holds a PhD in Environmental Communication from Surrey University. She is the recipient of 'Nepal Vidhya Bhushan', an educational accolade presented by the President of Nepal. Additionally, she is also a recipient of the 'Mahendra Vidhya Bhushan', a gold medal bestowed by the late King Birendra of Nepal, in recognition of her outstanding achievements in her master's degree in Anthropology.

A development communicator and a campaigner, Sangita works at an international development organisation based in London where she champions women's voices, sharing their stories through articles and blogs. She campaigns for women's rights to education worldwide. She has recently been awarded the prestigious 'Ambassador for Peace' award by the Universal Peace Federation for her contribution to international development sector.

Website: www.sangitaswechcha.com
Facebook: www.facebook.com/sangyshrestha
X: www.twitter.com/SangyShrestha
Email: sangyshrestha@hotmail.com

Rose's Odyssey

Tales of love and loss

If you have enjoyed this short story collection, please help other readers know about it by leaving a review on Amazon.

Printed in Great Britain
by Amazon

40087648R00108